The Alien Stranger

THE ALIEN STRANGER

BOB TICER

ReadersMagnet, LLC

The Alien Stranger
Copyright © 2022 by *Bob Ticer*

Published in the United States of America
ISBN	Paperback:		978-1-957312-81-1
ISBN	eBook:		978-1-957312-82-8

All rights reserved. No part of this publication may be reproduced, stored in a retrieval system or transmitted in any way by any means, electronic, mechanical, photocopy, recording or otherwise without the prior permission of the author except as provided by USA copyright law.

The opinions expressed by the author are not necessarily those of ReadersMagnet, LLC.

ReadersMagnet, LLC
10620 Treena Street, Suite 230 | San Diego, California, 92131 USA
1.619. 354. 2643 | www.readersmagnet.com

Book design copyright © 2022 by ReadersMagnet, LLC. All rights reserved.

Cover design by *Ericka Obando*
Interior design by *Dorothy Lee*

TABLE OF CONTENTS

1	Finding Life Purpose	7
2	Worlds Within Worlds	15
3	Another Encounter	29
4	Up And Over	37
5	Homicide Investigation	45
6	Thought To Thought	53
7	Proving Innocence	60
8	Strange Banking	66
9	Becoming A Spy	78
10	Real Wealth Economics	90
11	Summer Lake	97
12	Threat Arrives	108
13	Rehired	114
14	A Place To Hide	124
15	To The Rescue	129
16	The Game Begins	138

1
FINDING LIFE PURPOSE

Kayla was on her bicycle nearing the bike path across the street from Autzen stadium. As she turned onto the bike path, she noticed a hummingbird hovering high up in front of the forest of trees. It received too much of her attention for her to be aware of a guy running out of the forest towards her. She swerved to miss him and fell onto his chest. He wrapped his arms around her while stumbling backward to fall down on his back with his head hitting a rock.

"Owl!" he bellowed with his eyes squeezed tight and his hands above his ears.

She quickly got off his chest to sit beside him.

"Are you okay," she asked gazing and leaving her mouth wide open.

"I'll live," he answered with his hands at the back of his head. "How about you: Are you okay?"

"I'm fine."

"I'm so sorry I got in your way," he apologized. "I need to watch where I'm going."

"I'm sorry," she also apologized. "I saw a hummingbird. It got my attention; now you're hurt."

"I'll probably live. I feel pain in my head, but not in my arms and legs. Are you sure you're okay?"

"I don't know; am I?" she asked with a shrug.

He eyed her with a crinkled nose.

"You are with me," he replied still gazing at her face, "but it looks like you're missing an earring."

She placed her finger on her right earlobe.

"I'll find it," she replied.

They both got up and searched for it, but to no avail.

"It could've fallen off somewhere else," she finally confessed. "I accidentally stepped on it this morning and it didn't connect very well."

He reached inside a pocket for a pair of earrings.

"Take these."

She stood in awe gazing at them.

"Are you serious," she finally replied. "They have to be expensive."

"They're not," he replied shaking his head. "I was jogging yesterday and stopped nearby here to find out why some guy reached out to me with them in his hand. What the heck; I had twenty bucks to spare for the poor fellow."

"Aren't diamonds expensive?" Kayla asked staring at him with raised eyebrows.

"It's doubtful they're real. How they shine as well as they do I don't know, but I suspect they're fake for sure."

"Maybe they're stolen," she replied shaking her head. "Do you really want to give them to me?"

"I don't have any use for them," he replied with a shrug.

"Doesn't your girlfriend want them?"

"I don't have one. I'm still looking."

"You seem nice enough. There's no need for you to buy your way in. And, you don't owe me. I owe you for getting in your way."

He again shrugged.

"Sorry," she said, "I'm almost late for work. I need to leave right now. I thank you for saving me. Maybe we'll meet somewhere else."

"Where do you work?" he asked leaning his head slightly forward.

"I'm a waitress in the diner of Tommy's Inn that recently opened on Franklin Boulevard."

"I'd like to check it out. I just turned twenty one today and would like to celebrate at some place where I can enjoy a nice dinner."

"It'll be on me if you come."

"That's very nice of you, but I owe you for getting in your way."

"It was my fault," she loudly insisted. "I saw a hummingbird and wasn't looking where I was going."

"I was running too fast trying to get myself in shape for the upcoming season."

"Is that football? Are you a player?"

"Yes. I'm Bard Sucrets. The coach's office is just across the street. He sticks around for us."

"I think I've heard your name somewhere."

"Please take these earrings. I don't have any use for them."

"Okay. If you arrive at Tommy's Inn to get a free dinner on me, I'll take them."

"What if I bring my friends? Would they get one too?" he asked with raised eyebrows.

"How many do you have?"

"Just a few thousand," he kidded with a grin.

"I reckon I'll need to go to the bank to get a loan," she kidded back.

"If you take these earrings now, I'll promise to be there for a free meal."

"Thanks," she said after taking the earrings he handed her and then turning to get back onto her bicycle. "I'm looking forward to seeing you there enjoying a very good meal, but we might not have enough room for all your friends."

He shrugged. She waved goodbye continuing on her way. After a couple minutes she arrived at one of the bike bridges over the Willamette River. She noticed a hummingbird hovering on the other side a ways to the right. She wondered why they would be where there were no flowers to feed on. She did know some people used hummingbird feeders.

The bike path on the other side of the bike bridge converged to the left into a paved road leading to Franklin Boulevard. Although it was paved, it included a slight incline.

When she finally arrived at the inn, got off her bicycle and locked it to a bicycle rack, she again noticed a hummingbird hovering nearby. She gazed at it shaking her head with an open mouth and placing a hand on an earring. She suspected the hummingbird was following her for some reason connected to Bard and the earrings.

She walked on into the inn to stand before Thomas Olsen, the owner and manager.

"Sorry I'm late," she apologized. "My mother was in a lot of pain and I had an encounter along the way."

"You know," he replied while leaning slightly forward with a pointed finger, "I'll need more dependent service when this place finally starts filling up."

"I'll try my best to be on time," she promised. "Maybe I should get here an hour early."

"I have someone filling out an application. I want to see what she can do. Would you mind showing her?"

"No problem," Kayla replied nodding yes.

He turned to walk back into his office. She then walked into the diner to meet up with the cook who was covering for her.

"You're a little late today," Alice noted.

"It's been a strange day," Kayla replied with a shrug. "It's been haywire, and I'm not only late; Mr. Olsen wants me to show a new hire the ropes."

"Good luck," Alice said turning to walk into the kitchen.

Kayla took notice of the dining room. It was all in order ready to serve. There was nothing for her to do but to be ready to serve whatever few customers straggled in.

After she sat down at a table, she reached for the earrings Bard had given her and put them on as the owner approached with a color girl beside him.

"Nice earrings," the color girl noted.

"Some guy I had an encounter with across the street from Autzen stadium gave them to me. He said his name is Bard Sucrets and that he's a football player. We collided, and I was missing an earring."

"Wow," the color girl blurted, "he's the All-American who could've turned pro but decided to stay for his final year."

"Ooh," Kayla uttered, "It was sure nice to give me the earrings after he noticed I was missing one and we were unable to find it."

"That was nice of him," Mr. Olsen said.

"Yeah, I said I'd give him and his friends a free meal. He might have thousands of them. I sure hope they don't all come. I'll have to go to the bank and get a loan."

"You two get acquainted," Mr. Olsen said as he turned to walk away nodding while eying the ceiling.

"I'm Wanda Sue," she introduced herself. "I was just hired as a temp when needed."

"I'm Kayla. Have a seat. I'd like to find out what you know and how we might help each other."

"I know economics," she replied.

"Well," Kayla replied eying her. "I reckon you'll be in charge of the cash register."

They sat down at opposite sides of the table facing each other.

"I've waitressed before," Wanda Sue replied. "This is just temporary while I'm on summer break. I'm a student at the university majoring in economics?"

"How well do you know Bard?" Kayla asked.

"He's an All-American who could've turned pro," Wanda Sue reiterated, "but he's staying for his senior year believing the team could go all the way. I sure hope he's not hurt too bad."

"His head just landed on a rock," Kayla replied grimacing. "Hopefully he'll be okay and I won't get run out of town."

"I'm sure he will," Wanda Sue replied while nodding with eyes squeezed shut.

"Do you have a good plan in knowing what you want to do with your life," Kayla asked.

"I do. Don't you know what you want out of life?" Wanda Sue asked in turn.

"I want more control of it," Kayla revealed. "It's difficult when the world is against you."

"I'm not against you," Wanda Sue replied with a shrug, "and I know you're not against me just because of the color of my skin."

"Sorry," Kayla apologized. "You people have had an unfair burden placed on you for no justification whatsoever."

"Yep," Wanda Sue agreed while bowing and shaking her head, "it's been a challenge that has become more doable, and there are lots of problems for all of us to contend with. It's part of life. Haven't you had challenges to overcome as well? Aren't you going to further your education."

"It's difficult without having a scholarship," Kayla replied appearing sad bowing her head facing the floor. My dad was killed when I was fourteen. My mother has cancer and is in need of an expensive operation. Her uncle wants her to have it, but he has to sell his house in order to pay for it. We all live in it for now."

"Life can sure be a challenge for any of us," Wanda Sue replied nodding her head yes. "Can you afford rent or do you need to pay your fair share?"

"I now help out paying rent. My mother's uncle has social security. It's barely enough to pay his property taxes and such other costs as my mother's medical expenses, and he's growing old and could have some health problems of his own. I clean the house and help out anyway I can."

"He must be a nice guy."

"He's great," Kayla replied nodding, "and I want to be just as great."

"He's sure been a good influence on you."

Kayla shrugged nodding yes.

"What do you have in mind for the future?" Wanda Sue asked. "A community college isn't very expensive. I should've enrolled in one for my first two years of credits."

"I'm just trying to figure out why I'm here and what I need to do with my life."

"That's it?" Wanda Sue asked with a shrug. "What do you need to know?"

"I just want to know what I can do in life to be deserving of it. What do you plan to do with your education?"

"Hopefully I'll become an accountant and be able to pay off my student loan."

"Life can be tough," Kayla assured.

"It's a challenge for all of us. Even animals compete for food, and they even steal and kill for it if they have to."

"Is it worth it?" Kayla asked facing the floor with a frown.

"It seems to be so far. Maybe we just need to figure out how to respond to whatever happens."

"Well," Kayla replied, "the challenge here is not to get bored. So far there's only been a once in awhile drop-in. You'll likely only be on standby until needed."

"I probably should still look elsewhere, but, for today, what the heck?

2
WORLDS WITHIN WORLDS

Bard jogged out among trees and noticed one of his teammates sitting at a table beside a small pond at Alton Baker Park. He jogged over to sit beside the color guy. He slouched down facing the table with heavy breathings.

"How's it going?" Jack asked.

"I'm getting into better shape. I bumped my head on a rock a few hours ago, but I still got my arms and legs to run fast and catch the ball."

"Don't kill yourself. We have plenty of time before the season starts."

"I got in the way of a girl riding her bike on her way to work," Bard informed Jack. "She was in a hurry. I caught her and fell back hitting my head on that rock: How you doing?"

"I'm not sure," Jack replied. "A bird on that pond keeps calling me a quack, but that's not as bad as dogs calling me a wolf. I'm no wolf; I'm a nice guy."

"You're a duck," Bard replied in referring to the mascot name of the University of Oregon athletics.

"Did that girl get hurt?" Jack asked.

"No, but she lost an earring. I tried giving her new ones, but she wouldn't take them unless I promised to get a free meal at the diner where she works."

"That was nice of her. How nice is she?"

"She seems nice enough for me wanting to know her better. I planned on going there for that meal, but I don't think I have much left in me to make it there before it closes."

"I have my car," Jack offered.

"Do you want to join me for dinner?"

"Is mine free too?"

"I'll pay. It's my twenty first and I'd like to have some company."

"Hey, there's no need for you to pay for me. It's your birthday. Where is it?"

"It's that new place on Franklin Boulevard."

"You mean Tommy's Inn?"

"Yep . . . do you know something about it?"

"Wanda Sue said she was going to apply for a temporary waitress position there today."

"When do you want to go?" Bard asked.

"I'm ready, but I think you need rest up a little."

"Yep, I need a break from being bored. Did you get much out of that guy's physics' book you were reading?"

"It sure simplifies," Jack answered nodding yes. "It simplifies even the Pythagorean Theorem in geometrical form, and it's consistent with the possibility of all established theory. It combines instead of disproving them. Even big bang is combined with tired light. Instead of theory being against theory, he puts them together as one."

"How is big bang proven? How can all mass in the universe originate from a tiny speck much tinier than the smallest atom?"

"It's not proven or disproven. It's more of a continuation of theory. By the Planck constant, atomic mass–energy and its radius are constant. Smaller volume is thus more energy. That's consistent with Boyle's law whereby pressure multiplied by volume is a constant."

"Are you sure about that?"

"A volume of half radius is one-eighth smaller with one-fourth as much surface area. A particle in the smaller one moves half the distance to one-fourth surface area. That's eight times more pressure. It's thus constant."

"Yeah, almost zero volume is then almost of infinite mass-energy. Doesn't that conflict with Einstein's theory of more mass density becoming a black hole whereby nothing, including light, can escape? How could it then have expanded outward?"

"It's questionable but possible. Theory isn't fact. This guy that wrote the book only questions theoretical bias. Those theorists who believe all the mass and energy of the universe could've been contained within a tiny speck refuse such other possibilities as mass-energy being part of an ethereal medium that exists throughout space."

"How come we don't detect it?"

"It exists in various equilibrium states. Our adjustment to them just becomes how we perceive reality."

"Why's it needed?"

"How can we all perceive light moving at the same speed even though we move at different speeds relative to each other?" Jack asked back wide eyed and leaning his head forward.

"I don't know," Bard replied with a shrug. "It doesn't seem anymore possible than how all the mass-energy in the universe can fit into a volume of space much tinier than the smallest atom?"

"All possibilities are on the table," Jack said. "You just need to keep an open mind. Something could've created our universe the way it is, and there could be other creations we don't know about."

"Has he come up with anything?"

"A few things are interesting, like the gravitational constant divided by light speed equaling the Hubble constant."

Bard shrugged.

"He first figured it was just a mathematical coincidence even though it was exactly according to a Hubble constant of seventy kilometers a second at a distance away of one million parsecs. But, he finally realized that the units of measure that determine the value of the gravitational constant cancel out. The distance measure cancels out in view of centripetal acceleration divided by light speed. The mass measure cancels out in view of the Hubble constant being measured according to change in light energy."

"You know," Bard replied shaking his head in doubt, "I'm ready to go to the restaurant if you are."

"Let's go," Jack said getting up to lead Bard to the car.

When they arrived at and entered the diner, they saw only Kayla and Wanda Sue sitting at a table. They walked up to it.

"What are nice girls like you two doing in a place like this?" Bard asked facing Kayla.

"It's my job," Kayla replied. "What's an all-American doing here? Why didn't you turn pro?"

"Hey," he replied raising his eyebrows along with a curious expression, "you're a fan. I like that. I figured I need another year to get over my shyness and find my sweetheart. This could be the place."

Wanda Sue faced him grinning.

"I'm Wanda Sue looking for a guy like you."

"Well," Bard replied with a wink, "you seem very nice. I'm sure we'll have plenty of time to get to know each other, but I shy away from poets."

Kayla eyed him.

"I'm Kayla Chalet, not looking for a fray, but what can I say?"

He gazed narrow eyed slightly to his right.

"Hey," he finally replied, "show me the way to a nice fish filet and I'll be a poet someday."

"Good one," Kayla replied. "It just happens to be the special of the day. Is that just another coincidence?"

Mr. Olsen approached the table.

"Hello," he introduced himself. "I'm new to this area. I heard it's someone's birthday today. Would all four of you like to have free meals on the house?"

"Do dogs like to bark?" Jack asked.

Mr. Olsen gave a thumbs-up. Bard sat down beside Kayla.

"Hi Jack," Wanda Sue said to him when he seated himself beside her.

Kayla glanced at them.

"He's also on the football team," Wanda Sue said facing her. "We've been dating."

"Wow," Kayla replied, "another coincidence. There're sure been a lot of them today."

"I'd like to get to know you two," Mr. Olsen said facing Bard. "Do you mind if I join you all for a discussion?"

"Not at all," Bard replied.

"I'll get the menus," Kayla said standing up.

"Alice will be serving us," Mr. Olsen replied. "She doesn't have much to do right now."

Kayla, facing Mr. Olsen, nodded her head to the left. He got up to follow her away from the table as Alice approached it.

"Bard is the guy I bumped into earlier," she said to him. "He gave me these earrings, but I told him he gets a free meal on me, and kidded him that all the friends he brings also get one. I'm sure he knows I was just kidding."

"Well, I'm not kidding. The meals are on me. Don't you want to be part of it?"

She gazed at him with a slack-jaw.

"This is unreal. How can I mess up so much only to be awarded for it, and why is it I now see a hummingbird everywhere I go? I think it might have something to do with Bard and the earrings."

He shrugged.

"I don't know anything about the hummingbird, but Bard is no doubt popular with a large following."

"Yes," she agreed leaving her mouth open, "I completely understand, and I'll do all I can for him and all of his friends to have excellent dinners, but what if more customers happen to come in?"

"Alice can handle it. She doesn't have very much to do as of yet, and it'll be awhile before she does. Rooms will need to be preregistered when football season starts. We need to prepare for it, and having customers here now will help."

They walked back to the table where Alice stood ready to take orders.

"Does everyone want the special along with coffee?" Mr. Olsen asked.

When they all nodded yes, he pointed at Alice. Kayla and Wanda Sue followed her to the kitchen, and the latter two came back with coffee, cups, plates, silverware and so forth.

"What's being discussed?" Kayla asked after she and Wanda Sue sat back down after they had made a few more trips to the kitchen.

"What would you like to know?" Bard asked.

"I just want to know why I'm here and what I can do with my life," Kayla replied.

"What do we need to know?" Thomas Olsen asked. "How can we learn to do it? What is the real truth about the world we live in, and what is our real purpose in life? Why are some of us straightforward while some of us are more inclined to deflect with humor?"

"Being straightforward is like being brave," Kayla said. "Being humorous is defensive."

"Humor relieves stress," Bard replied eying the ceiling. "It's sure helped me in the locker room after a difficult workout, and it likely kept me out of a fight or two."

"Good answer," Wanda Sue noted. "It's directly related to emotion and can help relieve stress, but it can also be a means of avoiding responsibility. It can also be a way of releasing frustration on somebody, as to degrade them in attacking their personality."

"How can we overcome it?" Kayla asked.

"We'll need to be in harmony with common goals," Wanda Sue replied. "We compete to be in control of our own destinies, but if forces are too much for an individual to overcome, then we need to join efforts to succeed in a struggle for a common cause instead of just allowing the world to overcome individual incapability."

"How will it help me succeed?" Bard asked. "I need freedom to compete with my skills."

"Although you're free to play," Wanda Sue replied, "you need to comply with rules of the game, and of the coach's strategy to win as a team player. After all, you have teammates. If you don't help them when needed, you're more likely to lose."

"I am a team player, but what if I'm aware of something the coach isn't?"

"Civilization has evolved by means of learning," Jack noted. "One way has merely been to listen and accept whatever you've been told. It helps somewhat. Physics has had success with only mathematical formulation of theory without causal explanation, but knowing how birds fly helped us fly as well."

"How can the world exist?" Kayla asked. "Is it just some material substance that somehow just happens to exist in a way our minds can be aware of it? Is there a beginning and an end, or is it somehow all part of an infinite past and a forever future?"

"Good questions," Jack acknowledged. "Our finite way of thinking doesn't seem to allow us to perceive the answers, and what we do perceive as normal is a lot different than what has been learned according to theory."

"Why's that?" Bard asked. "You're majoring in physics and biochemistry. What's different of it than just living your life?"

"You shoot pool," Jack replied. "If you apply conservation of momentum, then you can predict where balls end up after collision. It's just particle effect, but particle effect isn't sufficient in itself to explain the cause of gravity. By conservation of momentum, what comes in is the same as what goes out."

"Isn't gravity explained?" Kayla asked.

"It can be," Jack answered, "but not as particle effect alone. There's a lot more of nature than just particles of mass."

"What else is there?" Bard asked. "Doesn't even light consist of particles?"

"It was interpreted as such after finding atoms were reflected back more from a metal when bombarded by light of a higher frequency instead of more intensity, but frequency is also a wave property. Waves can explain all particle effects plus effects particles do not explain. Not explained is how a single particle can pass through one of two holes and result in a wavelike interference effect."

"How can waves be what they are without particles?" Bard asked. "Isn't ocean water filled with particles?"

"How can particles exist as particles," Jack asked with his arms slung up and out. What keeps them intact?"

Bard shrugged with a crinkled nose.

"What's the problem?" Kayla asked.

"The problem is theoretical bias," Jack replied facing her. "The ether as a medium for wave action is dismissed in believing particle action is the norm, but the particle needs some kind of force to hold it together, such as radiation, which light is. If it too is of particles, then what holds them together?"

"So," Bard said. "What do you propose?"

"It's more complicated. A medium is needed. An ethereal medium necessary for wave effect had and is still being considered by some theorists, but the real problem is the close minded establishment of most students and professors. They accept only what they have been told or taught. I now know more than them after reading with an open mind a book written by someone who self educated himself."

"Wasn't the ether disproven?" Bard asked.

"No. It's just been ignored. Newton believed it would interfere with planets' motion. Einstein disregarded it for just being unnecessary for a mathematical formulation of theory. Successful equations of wave mechanics were merely reinterpreted as probability conditions. It's that theoretical bias. There are Newtonians and whoever that just won't allow the development of other theory. They'd be a lot less naive if they just opened their minds."

"So," Bard asked, "why do we need waves?"

"Particles interact to produce wave effects, and waves comply with the laws of momentum and energy, but they also result in effects that are additional to particle effects alone."

"Like what?" Bard asked.

"Different particles aren't able to occupy the same space whereas waves superimpose. They can even become invisible by way of maintaining states of equilibrium for the world to become a lot more complex than how it's normally perceived as that of shooting pool. Some of it could even be invisible to us."

"Hey, Alice," Bard said facing her as she was filling coffee cups, "have you been to Wonderland yet?"

She grinned while shaking her head no.

"I'd like to go with you," Kayla also kidded.

"How does this wave action explain gravity?" Mr. Olsen asked facing Jack. "Couldn't particles become smaller to more easily escape?"

"It hasn't been shown to comply with conservation of momentum," Jack answered. "There is this second law of thermodynamics called entropy that specifies a particular condition of energy. Such energy states of equilibrium do not allow disorder to occur among them. Two objects of the same temperature don't change the temperature of the other even if one contains more heat, as the humidity of water has more heat at a lower temperature."

"So," Bard asked, "How does it work with gravity?"

"According to Einstein's Special Relativity there is a principle of covariance. All observers perceive themselves relatively at rest if they don't accelerate. Light speed is the same for them all even though they move relative to it. How this is perceived as such is by means of equilibrium states being according to how we can adjust to them. Light reflects or passes through according to equilibrium states of relative motion. Its how gravity is conditional as well. Waves of it are only minutely reflected while parts of them move on through the medium in maintaining the equilibrium states."

"That's a very good possibility," Mr. Olsen acknowledged, "but are waves really needed?"

"Particles can form into wave action," Jack reiterated. "Ocean waves are an example, but the equilibrium state is still needed in order for the momentum to pass through undetected."

Alice arrived with a couple plates of fish filets, placing them in front of Bard and Jack.

"More are on their way," she said along with more coffee or whatever else you would like to have."

"There must be a lot more than just the visible world we live in," Kayla noted facing Jack."

"Yep," Jack agreed. "How is existence itself possible? How can we even be aware of it? How can it just exist with no beginning and no end?"

"I only care to know the physics of shooting pool," Bard said. "It's the world I live in."

"How does a polar bear know its meal is ten miles away beneath a thick layer of ice?" Jack asked. "Why did a cat raise its head when the car approached close to where it had lived before being taken to a place more than a thousand miles away?"

"What can we know for sure?" Kayla asked.

"Some things are seemingly beyond our finite minds," Jack replied. "There could be more possibilities that we're unaware of, such as higher states of consciousness than our subconscious. Although we aren't likely able to explain all of it, there is still more we could know about, but we need to do it with open minds."

"Minds are politically closed as well," Wanda Sue noted. "Extreme conservatives in favor of the rich refuse to let change occur. The rich being in control want to stay in control instead of allowing for more opportunity for others to compete. Although roads are social by way of government allowing for the transport of more wealth, and even though free education has been instrumental for innovative ways to create better living conditions, there'd be no social security without those with open minds that were willing to promote it."

"She's a socialist," Bard said facing Jack. "I think my freedom is in jeopardy. I might not even get to choose who to play for next year."

"Wouldn't our freedom be in jeopardy if ten guys were able to buy all homes and dictate how we can rent to live in them?" Wanda Sue asked with a sneer.

"It'd be up to us to comply or revolt," Bard replied.

"What if they got elected and took over the nuclear program?" Wanda Sue asked.

"They wouldn't get my vote," Bard again countered.

"They wouldn't get mine either," Wanda Sue sort of agreed. "I'm sure there'd be a revolt with lots of chaos, and they might just decide to use those nuclear weapons."

"Well," Mr. Olsen said. "We're having a very good discussion. You all have very good ideas that should be shared. A social club is warranted. I propose we start one here and now. Would you all want to participate?"

They all nodded yes. He got up to walk back to his office. Jack got up to leave. Bard remained seated.

"I just want to say goodbye," Bard said to Jack

"Good luck," Jack replied eying the ceiling,

Kayla approached as Jack walked out the door,

"You must want your earrings back," she conjectured.

"No," Bard said shaking his head. "It's just that I don't want to leave without saying goodbye. Thanks for the free meals. Did the owner really give them to us or do you now have to do something extra?"

"No. he wants customers to know he's here for them. Just like he said, they were on him."

"I'll be back, and I'm sure Jack will too along with some of our other friends."

"That'll be great."

"I like you," he admitted, "and I'd like to be your friend and get to know you a lot better."

"I like you too, and I hope to see you again, and I need to ask you a question."

"I'm not married."

"No, it's about hummingbirds and earrings. I kept seeing one just before and after we met. There were no flowers for it to feed on."

"They must be getting fed by people in the area," he suggested.

"Thanks! I guess that'll have to do for now. I sort of suspect it's somehow connected to the earrings you gave me. I think it was the same hummingbird following me."

"Okay," he said with a shrug while getting up to leave, "hope to see you sooner than later."

3
ANOTHER ENCOUNTER

Kayla was on her bicycle and heading home. She peddled with ease on down the slope of the back road, and she noticed a hummingbird hovering in front of the bike bridge when she approached it. She shook her head wondering about its presence. It remained close by even when she crossed over the bridge to enter the wooded area on the other side of the river.

The wooded area of tall trees barely allowed enough light for her to see more than a short distance in front of her. Barely was she able to break soon enough to avoid running over a fellow lying on the bike path.

She lowered the kickstand and crouched down beside the guy's head to find out if he was alive. She noticed he was breathing.

"Are you okay?" she asked when he opened his eyes.

She reached for her phone after he nodded.

"No," he bellowed. "I'm okay. Don't call anyone."

"You need to get off the path. I'll help you."

He struggled to get up on his knees and to his feet, and then staggered about. She pulled on his arm to guide him to a grassy area near a pond. Streams and ponds were abundant in the area that was considered to be part of Alton Baker Park: it still being city property.

He suddenly staggered about in front of her placing his arms around to her backside. They toppled to the ground with him on top of her.

"Hey babe, are you okay?" he asked still on top of her.

"Thanks," she shouted with a crinkled nose, "I'll live. Can I get up?"

"I'm sorry. Can you spare a couple dollars? I'm about to starve to death. I've had nothing to eat all day."

"Sorry," she replied while attempting to get up onto her feet, "I left my purse at home."

She trembled feeling his hand on her shoulder pushing her back down onto her back.

"It's a nice hot night for a swim, don't you think?" he asked nodding with raised eyebrows.

"Are you crazy?" she asked with a fixed gaze.

"Let's have a little fun."

"No thanks," she replied with a crinkled nose. "I'm in a hurry to get home and find out how my mother is doing. She has cancer."

Kayla tried to get back up on her feet, but the fellow pushed her back down and covered her mouth with his hand. She reached for her phone she had in a cloth container strapped to one side of her. He grabbed it away from her with his other hand and threw it.

She tried to scream for help, but to no avail with his hand on her mouth.

"Nice earrings rich girl; I'm sure you don't need them as much I do right now."

"Take them," she briefly became able to cry out by jerking her head to the right. "I don't want them."

"You also need to slow down to have some fun. I'll show you how, babe."

"Get off me," she was barely able to say.

She felt helpless pushing to no avail against his weight and his hand covering her mouth to block it from any attempt to scream.

He ripped open her blouse.

"Please," she was suddenly able to cry out, "don't hurt me."

He had suddenly fallen after tearing her blouse, to lay flat on the ground right beside her.

"Is he dead?" she asked a fellow about five feet six inches tall she suddenly noticed standing a few feet away holding a barrel like device similar to a pen.

"I only sedated him," he calmly replied. "He will wake up in about five or ten minutes."

"Who are you?" she asked narrow eyed.

"I am a stranger."

"Thanks stranger. Can you call the police?"

"I can call the police, but I prefer not to call them."

"Why's that?" she asked rubbing her forehead.

"I am not a citizen here, and I could be arrested and detained by the police for having no proper identification to show them."

"You're an alien too?" she asked with a furrowed brow.

"Your statement is correct. I am here as an alien stranger."

"Well, alien stranger, it was sure nice of you to save me from being raped, and probably killed."

"I saved your life because of it being the proper thing to do, but I also need your help. This body I have grown here needs proper nutrition. Leaves, blackberries and tall grass are healthy enough food to sustain it, but I desire to experience more of what life here on this planet called Earth offers me. Money seems to be what provides more interesting adventure with more freedom to explore it."

"You poor thing," she replied with steady eye contact. "How can I help?"

He reached into his pocket and brought out a necklace.

"I will escort you to where you need to go if you do me a favor."

"What's that?" she asked eying him and not wanting to believe the worse.

"Will you sell this necklace for me? You can keep half of the money you receive for it. I only need a little bit of food to eat that you can buy for me with the other half."

The necklace he held in his hand contained shiny diamond like stones. She got up onto her feet and gazed at it.

"It's nice looking. It must be very expensive. Isn't it? What do you think it's worth?"

"I do not know what its monetary value is. I just need enough money to enjoy my visit here in this area where people tend to respect you more if you have money to spend."

"Yeah, they want it for sure. Where are you staying?"

She doubted it was a real diamond necklace, but what the heck: He had saved her from being raped, and she suspected he was the same guy who sold Bard the earrings she was wearing.

"The place where I normally stay at is a secret that I do not even want you to know of its location. The diamond earrings you now wear will reveal to me your presence."

"Yeah, they will, to you and everyone else, but why near here? Do you live close by?"

"Sorry. I do not want you or anyone else to know where I live, but I do need someone in particular that I can trust to purchase particular things for my needs. I am confident I can trust you with this necklace."

She glanced to her right with tight lips.

"So, you want to use me to sell your stuff. That could get complicated and be illegal, and I don't want to break the law."

"You are correct. Working for me and earning a large sum of money will require taxation if it becomes noticeable of your bank account. Still, you will have more additional income that is more than the tax you have to pay, and you can report it as a donation. Do you have a bank account that can receive donations?"

"I do. Why do you ask?"

"I need to donate it to you for you to be able to purchase more items for me."

"Sorry. I'm not going to divulge information on how to access it."

"I need essentials for healthy living and for knowing how to interrelate with the community of local residents. I am sure the expenses will not be too costly a burden to you. You will earn enough profit from your involvement to pay for your tax requirement."

"This is getting serious," she replied staring at him, "and I do need more income. I'll give it a go only if you assure me we're not breaking the law, and that this is not a scam."

"You can keep the necklace, as for now, and just provide me with only what is affordable to you, even if it is only food grown in a garden."

She shrugged tilting her head in disbelief.

"When and where do you want me to give you the stuff?"

"Anytime of day or night will be okay with me. Just hide it right here in the bushes. I will be aware of you leaving it, and I will be able to get to it before anyone or anything else does."

"Okay, we have an agreement. Thanks, but I can get home by myself. See you later."

He reached out with something in his hand.

"I believe this belongs to you."

"Thanks a lot," she said recognizing what he handed to her was her phone, "and I promise I won't call the police right away. You'll have all the time you need to get back to your hideout. I'm only calling them because that guy has a problem that needs to be taken care of. I don't want him to harm anyone else."

"Please do not call the police at all. I do not want this incident reported to them. He is only a problem now because he had taken addictive opioids as medicine for his heartburn that confused his way of thinking."

"You must know him well."

"Yes, I do know him. He has been trying to help me, and I have been trying to help him."

"Okay, I'll give both you and him the benefit of doubt for now, but if something happens to someone else, I might need to report it."

"I appreciate your honesty, and I trust that you will do what you just promised me you will do."

She waved goodbye while walking to her bicycle and shaking her head in disbelief.

"Goodbye Miss Kayla Chalet," he replied.

With one foot on the bicycle peddle and the other on the ground, she waited a few seconds puzzled before turning to ask how he knew her name, but he was nowhere to be seen.

She stood puzzled as to why someone as well dressed as he was would peddle jewelry in the woods and be able to disappear so fast.

She also felt uncomfortable where she was at. She was eager to be on her way. When the guy who had attempted to rape her got up onto his feet, she quickly got onto her bike and peddled hard to get as far away as she could for him to have no chance whatsoever to catch up to her, and she leaned forward hoping that she would be able to avoid running over anyone else that might be on the bike path.

She soon arrived at the road where Autzen Stadium was on the other side. The way home to the right was more visible and safe without trees blocking light from stars and the moon.

She again noticed a hummingbird hovering nearby. The alien stranger had told her to wear the earrings for him to know her whereabouts. It indicated they were somehow connected and of advanced technology.

She finally arrived home to put her bicycle into a lockup shed behind the house, and again she noticed the hummingbird hovering nearby. She went to the backdoor, entered the house, and expected to find Donald and Darcy watching TV, but they did not appear to be home.

A paper note was on her bedroom door. Her mother had been taken to the hospital in an ambulance. Donald rode his bicycle. She frowned after reading it.

"What a day," she said to herself. "I almost got raped only to then come home and find out my mother is now in the hospital, and it seems I'm being spied on by that guy's hummingbird. I'm sure he now knows where I live."

She went on into her bedroom, took off the earrings and laid them beside the necklace on the dresser. She gazed at them for awhile before undressing to retire for the night.

Although she had her phone and considered calling the police for the sake of future safety of all other bicyclists, she decided against it. After all, she had made a promise to the alien stranger. He had rescued her, and she now felt she owed him something in turn. Hopefully, he was not just using her to peddle stolen property.

4
UP AND OVER

When Kayla got out of bed and dressed, she decided to wear the earrings Bard had given her, and she put the necklace in her purse before leaving her bedroom. Her mother's uncle was in his lazy boy chair watching the morning news on television when she entered the living room.

"How's my mother doing?"

"She needs that operation. I might have to sell the house."

"Maybe not," she replied standing close by and pointing at one of the earrings. "This place where I'm working is about to boom."

Donald leaned slightly forward gazing at her.

"They're sure nice looking. What the heck is going on?"

"A nice guy gave them to me. Do you know who Bard Sucrets is?"

Donald sat shaking his head with his mouth open in disbelief.

"Are you sure it was him? You could be getting yourself in big trouble."

"It was him. The owner of the inn where I work gave us and his friend free dinners."

"That sounds serious," Donald noted. "How long have you known each other?"

"I bumped into him yesterday. He was running fast while I watched a hummingbird."

"Well, I can't blame you for liking him, and I surely can't blame him for liking you."

"Yeah, but the big deal is the owner wanted me to please Bard for him to spread the word. Bard gave me the earring because I was missing one after I ran him over with my bike. He seemed to be a nice guy wanting to share his wealth."

"That sounds good, but don't make it a habit. You should watch where you're going."

"You're right. On my way home I almost ran over another guy lying on the bike path, and I ended up with a necklace as well as these earrings."

She reached for the necklace in her purse.

"Wow," he blurted out, "running over a guy turns out to be a good thing for you."

"The necklace was given to me by someone else who recued me from being raped by the guy I almost ran over. He wants me to sell it for him. He said he only wants food for it, and he said he'll put money in my bank account so that I can buy other stuff for him."

Donald stared at her with an open mouth.

"Did you call the police?"

"No," Kayla replied shaking her head, "the guy who saved me is an alien. He doesn't want to be caught and deported."

"You still need to call the police."

"He rescued me. I owe him."

"Are those real diamonds?" Donald asked.

Kayla shrugged.

"Why would a guy give an expensive necklace away to someone he just met for very little profit?" Donald asked pointing at her.

Kayla shrugged again.

"They could be worth twenty years," Donald warned.

"I owe him. He rescued me from that guy."

"Are you sure they weren't in cahoots?"

"He sedated him."

Donald eyed the ceiling.

"Why did he just happen to have something to sedate someone with at the moment?"

"I don't know. Maybe he's just all alone and doesn't want to be deported. This area nearly leads the nation in its homeless population. He could be desperate in need of help by someone he's able to trust and needs something to protect himself from those he cannot trust."

"You still need to call the police," Donald insisted. "If they're not stolen, there's no need for him to worry. If they were, then you could be an accessory. It could be on record even if you don't get convicted."

"I'm not selling it. He gave it to me and I'm giving it back to him with food mostly from our garden."

"Well," Donald agreed, "not allowing him to use you is okay, I guess. I sure hope he's not a scammer. You'll need to protect yourself from whatever he's up to. I can escort you to work."

"What can I do?" Kayla asked with a shrug. "If he scams someone, I'll feel guilty for it. If he's just trying to be helpful, I'll feel guilty for getting him into trouble. He also retrieved my phone."

Donald shook his head while Kayla walked to the kitchen, turned the stove burner on medium, placed a kettle on top of it, opened the icebox, and reached for milk to pour into the kettle. She then added teaspoons of cinnamon, nutmeg, ginger, raisins and sesame seeds. She finally added enough oats and a sliced banana for Donald and her to have a nutritious breakfast.

She reached up into the cupboard for a bottle of vanilla while the oats were cooking. She walked over and gave it to Donald. He sipped a small amount of it to flush around in his mouth before being swallowed.

"If he puts money in my bank account," she said, "we could afford vanilla candles that are more effective in controlling your allergies."

"Don't tell me you're informing him."

"It's only a possibility if it turns out he has been telling the truth."

He frowned shaking his head.

After they finished their oatmeal breakfast, Kayla went outside to the garden for tomatoes and other vegetables for her to take to the alien stranger along with a sausage she had gotten out of the icebox. She placed them all in a basket above the rear wheel of her bicycle."

She peddled to where she had been rescued. She then hid the food and necklace within the bushes.

There was a hummingbird hovering nearby. She believed it belonged to the alien stranger, and when she got back onto her bicycle to continue on her way to work, she noticed him approaching from the opposite direction.

"I appreciate you bringing me food," he said. "Why did you not keep the necklace?"

She gazed at him with an open mouth wondering how he knew about the necklace.

"Sorry," she apologized. "I'm committed to taking care of my mother and her uncle. I cannot be involved in something like this. How did you know I brought it back?"

He pointed at the hummingbird. She began nodding her head in response.

"It could be helpful to your financial needs," he then replied.

"I'm sure someone else would be more deserving of it and a lot more helpful to you."

He stared slightly to her left. She turned to see the guy who seemingly tried to rape her.

"You owe me you damn alien," he bellowed while holding up a knife pointing towards them. "You're going to pay for not paying me."

The alien stranger turned and ran towards the bike bridge. The guy with the knife chased after him passing by Kayla. She then got back onto her bicycle to peddle as fast as she could to follow and keep up with them.

The alien stranger arrived at the bike bridge and continued on his way across it.

A few path goers on foot were coming the other way. One was running to pass ahead of them. He and the alien stranger seemed to have collided. Whether or not there was a collision, the alien stranger suddenly rose way up very high above the other guy to then dive down into the river. He surfaced to float downstream with the river current.

The other guy had stumbled backwards. He scuttled to the other side of the bridge leaning forward and staring in the direction of the current.

Kayla recognized him. It was Bard. She had a crush on him, but he now seemed to be more brutal like her dad was whenever coming home intoxicated and abusing her mother.

She felt helpless sitting on her bicycle wondering why Bard was on the bridge, and why he had heaved the alien stranger into the river. She didn't want to believe Bard was somehow involved, but she could not keep from thinking he had some reason to get even with the alien stranger. It occurred to her he might be doing drugs along with that other guy that had been chasing the alien stranger.

The fellow that had been chasing the alien stranger stood in front of the bridge. He turned around and walked back towards her. Although witnesses were present, she trembled when he approached close to her with knife in hand.

"Good luck," he said while walking past her seemingly with no remorse whatsoever.

She let out a sigh of relief, but she was still troubled by the event that just happened. She also noticed a fellow standing on the other side of the bridge having a camera pointing at Bard. The guy lowered his camera and held up his phone.

She noticed a hummingbird hovering above a lower east-west bike path closer to the river. It seemed determined to get her attention. She circled down to her left to arrive at the lower bike path from which she was able to approach the hummingbird.

It had not left. She continued towards it. It retreated a little ways to the west, indicating to her that it wanted her to follow it. She obliged feeling responsible for possibly saving a life.

She suspected it was a drone. It indicated the alien stranger had advanced technology. It further indicated the alien stranger was something other than just an alien hiding out to not be discovered and deported.

Although she now suspected the hummingbird was a drone, whoever was in control of it at the moment other than the alien stranger appeared to be another mystery. Did the alien stranger have help to find and rescue him? The other help could either be good or bad: good if it kept Bard out of trouble, but bad if it enabled the alien stranger and his cohorts more power to control her life.

It still appeared she was needed to save the alien stranger's life. She continued to follow the hummingbird just for the possibility she might be able to do it.

After awhile along the bike path the hummingbird hovered directly in front of her, and it darted now and then to her left.

Was it telling her something?

It was a bushy area having no clear path to the river. She got off her bicycle, walked with it about halfway to the river before leaving it.

She spotted someone under water beneath a fallen tree. It seemed hopeless that he would still be alive, but whoever controlled the drone probably knew more than she did. Whoever it could be could also be in need of help to save a life. She was still feeling obligated to do whatever she could to help do it.

She managed to go down into the cold water while leaving her shoes and purse behind. With barely enough strength, she managed to free him from underneath the log to lift him above the surface and pull him to shore where he lay motionless without breathing. She then lied down beside him feeling too tired to get up, but she struggled to rise to the occasion in trying to revive him. She pushed on his chest, but to no avail.

She felt helpless in need of assistance. She reached inside her purse for her cell phone and pushed nine-eleven buttons, but with no result of an answer or even a dial tone.

She felt faintish from the cold water having drained much of her heat energy. She tried to get up onto her feet but passed out during the effort to fall down and lie on the ground next to the alien stranger.

5
HOMICIDE INVESTIGATION

"Hello George," lady Detective Bentley said. "What are you doing here at the hospital? I can only wonder."

"I was at the bridge needing a good story to report. Bard had been jogging across it to get into shape. I got it all on camera and I was the one who called 911. I'm not merely a journalist: I'm your main witness."

"You are going to cooperate in keeping your lips sealed?" she asked nodding.

"You know I always have," he replied while nodding as well.

She nodded her head to the left to signal him to follow her on into the room where a doctor stood beside a patient.

"Is she going to make it?" Detective Bentley asked while showing her ID to the doctor.

"She's just unconscious. She'll be waking up any moment."

"Did she have any identity on her?"

"The policemen who carried her to the ambulance said they had searched the area and weren't able to find anything."

"What else do you know?"

George with phone in hand began pushing its buttons. Her phone rang. After answering it, she watched its screen while listening to a recording of the event:

"Did you heave that guy into the river?" she saw and heard a policeman asking Bard during the investigation at the bridge.

"No," Bard blurted his denial, "he jumped. I was just trying to get out of his way. I reckon he was trying to get out of my way. We collided and he jumped. I don't know how he went that high, but he did."

"That's way too high according to the other witnesses," the policeman noted.

"Yes," Bard slightly agreed, "it's too high to heave that much weight as well."

"You're big and strong," a policewoman said. "The witnesses claim he was a lot smaller than you."

"He was still too big for me to throw him that high."

"Have you been doing drugs," she asked.

"No, and I'll take a lie detector test."

The policewoman answered her phone.

"They spotted a body on the shore from the helicopter," she said facing the policeman. "It's on the shore. Searchers have been notified. They're almost there."

She held the phone and waited.

"It's a girl," she finally said. "She's still alive, only unconscious."

"Could it have been a girl instead of a guy," the policeman asked.

"She's soaking wet," the policewoman said about a minute later.

"Does she have any identity of who she is?" the policeman asked.

"They've found no purse or anything in her pockets to identify her, but she's wearing diamond like earrings."

"No," Bard blurted before slapping his palm on top of his forehead. "That can't be Kayla."

"Do you know her?" the policewoman asked.

"I don't think it's her. Yesterday, I gave this girl diamond like earrings after we collided on the bike path. I bought the earrings from a guy peddling them the day before. I think that was the guy who jumped into the river."

"We sure do want you to take the lie detector test," the policeman said.

When Kayla, lying in bed, opened her eyes, the detective beside her hung up the phone.

"Are you okay?" the doctor asked.

There was a pause.

"Hello," the detective greeted Kayla. "I'm here to ask you a few questions about what happened to you. I'm Detective Bentley."

"I have other patients I need to attend to," the doctor said.

"Do you know what happened?" the detective asked Kayla after the doctor walked on out of the emergency room. "What is your name?"

"I'm Kayla Chalet," she answered, "but I'm not sure what happened."

"Did someone throw you into the river?"

"I don't know. Was I in the river when you found me?"

"No, but you were on the bank soaking wet."

"I guess I wasn't thrown in the river, then."

"Why were you soaking wet?"

"I was in the river, but not thrown."

"We were searching for some guy who went into the river off a bike bridge. It appeared to be according to witnesses that he was thrown. You were found instead wet with no ID. It appears you could've been the victim. Maybe you were another victim."

"I found the guy in the river trapped under a fallen tree. I managed to go in and pull him to shore. I tried calling 911, but my cell phone didn't have a dial tone. I tried reviving him but wasn't able to. I got weak and passed out."

"There was no phone or ID found near you."

"Was my bike there?"

"No bicycle was found. You said you went to find the guy. Did you know him?"

"I met him last night."

"Do you know the guy who threw him in the river?"

"Yeah, it's Bard. I met him yesterday. He gave me earrings. Some guy wanted them. He tried raping me and was chasing the guy that saved me and jumped off the bridge."

"Those on you appear to be expensive diamonds. Why would he give them to you?"

"It was a replacement. I lost one."

"Why would he just happen to have them?"

"I don't know. He said he had bought them a day earlier from some guy peddling them. I believe he's the same guy that jumped into the river."

"How did you find him? It was in the police report that the area where you were found isn't visible from the bike path."

"I was guided by a hummingbird."

"What?" the detective bellowed.

"It was following me around after Bard gave me the earrings. I believe it's a drone."

"Are you willing to take a lie detector test?"

"Do I have to?"

"No, but it now appears you're obviously involved in a crime, and you could be guilty of a cover-up."

"My mother is here in the hospital. I'd like to see how she's doing."

"I'll be right back."

George followed the detective outside the emergency room.

"Are you getting enough of a good story on this one?" she asked him.

"It could go viral," he replied.

"Is her name really what she claims it is?"

"It's Kayla Chalet. Besides Bard knowing it, a missing report was filled by a Donald Hodges claiming to be her mother's uncle. He said she didn't show up for work and that some guy had tried to rape her the night before."

"What do you think is going on?" Detective Bentley asked.

"What do you think it is?" George asked.

"It appeared she was just another victim. It now appears she's trying to cover-up, claiming to be led by a drone disguised as a hummingbird. She knows Bard and claims he gave her diamond earrings that the drone detects."

"Can you prove she's lying?"

"Her statements make little sense. I'm sure I can get her to take a lie detector."

"You have another lead, don't you?"

"I know you know I do. Do I get your cooperation?"

"You know you do. Her claim of her mother being in the hospital is true. I was here earlier taking note of it. Donald came to visit his niece, which is her needing surgery for cancer. She's in room 312."

"I'll check it out. He could be up there knowing something, and it could be motive for her down here being involved in illegal activity."

"I'd like to go up with you."

"Don't you want to get what you can from Kayla?"

"Right now the priority is on the third floor."

They went up the elevator to the third floor and on into room 312.

The detective faced Donald to introduce herself.

"Hello. I'm Detective Bentley investigating a possible homicide. Kayla Chalet was found alive, brought here to the emergency room and is okay."

"Thank you," Donald replied. "I'm sure glad to here she's okay, but what happened?"

"It appears she tried to save some guy that went off the bridge into the river. Do you know anything about it?"

"I believe she was being scammed. She was given a diamond necklace by a guy. He tried to get her to do stuff for her after he supposedly saved her from being raped, and Bard had given her diamond earrings. They were most likely stolen and I suspect drugs are involved."

"The records show Bard passed a physical with no indication of any drug or medical usage of any kind, but that was a year ago."

"Some guy attempted to rape her last night. She said she was saved by the guy that gave her the necklace. I think they're in cahoots."

"What?" Kayla's mother blurted.

"What do you know about the hummingbird drone?" Detective Bentley asked facing Donald.

"I think they're putting her on. I don't know what Bard has to do with it, but it looks to be he's now off the team. I sure hope Kayla doesn't get run out of town for it."

"We'll try not to reveal her name, but she's a suspect and reporters are inquiring."

"Yeah," Donald replied grimacing. "Thanks. I know George here. Hopefully, he'll comply."

Detective Bentley waved goodbye as he and George began their return to the emergency room.

"Donald is on the third floor with your mother," Detective Bentley notified Kayla. "He said some guy attempted to rape you. Why didn't you report it?"

"A guy who saved me didn't want me to. He said the guy was on drugs. The guy who saved me was also the guy going into the river. That other guy was chasing him with a knife. Being chased is why he collided with Bard. He only was trying to save himself. Bard just defended himself. It was just an accident caused by the chaser."

"Why didn't you report the rape attempt?"

"The guy that saved me claims he's an alien that could be deported. He and the other guy were helping each other, and I didn't want to get someone that saved me into trouble."

"Do you have any idea where we could find them?"

"No. They're keeping it a secret, even from me."

"You could be involved in a possible homicide, and I'm sorry to have to tell you that inquiring reporters are doing their jobs. I'd like to keep your name secret while investigating. Are you willing to take a lie detector?"

"Okay, I'll take it. I'm sure it'll believe me."

6
THOUGHT TO THOUGHT

Kayla was escorted home after she took the lie detector. Donald had already retired for the night. She retired for the night as well to wake up the next morning to dress and feel sad with barely enough courage to walk out of her bedroom.

Kayla walked up to Donald sitting in his lazy boy chair. She stood gazing at her phone and purse on the table before him.

"They were on the porch by the front door," Donald informed her. "Your bicycle was somehow put back in the shed."

She picked up her purse and opened it. She then pulled the necklace out of it.

Donald just sat gazing. She just stood shaking her head with a crinkled nose.

"What's going on?" Donald finally asked.

"I don't know, but I'm going to find out."

"It was just reported on the news of someone going into the river. They believe it could be a homicide. No names were given, but they have witnesses, and I'm sure the word is getting out. You and Bard appear to be in lots of trouble. Your boss called to inform you that you're laid off. You should've gone to the police like I said. I was being questioned last night at the hospital by a detective. Darcy heard it."

"You're right. I'm not only out of a job; I'm about to get run out of town. I just cooperated. It was supposed to have been kept secret."

Donald bowed his head and rubbed his forehead.

"I could get a reverse mortgage, but when I pass on, it'll need to be paid off for you and your mom to have the house."

"Do what you need to do. My problem is my problem."

"What are you going to do about it?" Donald asked shaking his head with eyes closed tight.

"Well," she replied lifting up the necklace, "I need to find out why the guy wants me to have this."

Donald shook his head disgustingly.

"Maybe they want me to wear it instead of selling it," she speculated.

"That makes no sense?" Donald said.

"Neither does a hummingbird following me around when I wear the earrings," she replied.

Donald stared at her with an open mouth.

Kayla picked up her phone and walked back into her bedroom. She placed the necklace around her neck while facing a mirror on the wall. She soon bowed her frowning face.

She wondered if she should get rid of it.

"You need to keep it," she thought.

"No," she thought. "I don't want it."

"You need to wear it for me," she thought.

She was puzzled by her own thoughts.

"You need not be confused," she thought. "I can help you understand what you are thinking about. We need to meet somewhere in person for a better understanding of the situation."

"What," she blurted out loud enough for anyone in the house to hear. "Who and where are you? Are you in my mind? Have I gone insane?"

"I am who you refer to as the alien stranger communicating to you from my secret location. I am detecting thoughts from you and channeling my thoughts to you. You have not gone insane."

"Are you okay?" she heard Donald ask right outside her room.

"Hopefully I'm about to find out what's going on," she replied.

"What's going on?" he asked.

"It's insane. I'm not insane. Maybe I am. I seem to be in some kind of another world."

"I know you're not insane, but you do seem confused. You should get some mental help."

"Just try to be patient and I'll let you know what's going on as soon as I can figure it out."

"Okay," he replied. "I'll let it be for now, and I'm still willing to help in anyway I can."

"Thanks. That itself does help."

She felt somewhat guilty for being unwilling to accept his help, but she also felt he was unwilling to accept what she was experiencing as the real truth.

"How are you doing this?" Kayla thought to ask. "Why aren't you dead as you appeared to be when I found you?"

"Diamonds of the necklace are transformers amplifying brain energy in allowing the detection of your thoughts. I am not dead because I turned myself off because of the circumstantial threat to my life, and I have also increased the monetary value of your banking account with the use of your phone for needed information. I did it to reward you for rescuing me from under the log."

"Why did you need me to rescue you?" she thought to ask.

"When I was safe on shore, my drone alerted me to turn myself back on. I then left from the area in order for me not to be discovered. I was barely able to do it."

"You left me passed out on the ground and took my stuff. What if they hadn't found me?"

"I apologize for that, but I had stayed hidden in the bushes to make sure you would be found and rescued. You were only passed out, and you were spotted by someone in a helicopter. When the police were close on their way to rescue you, I needed them to be redirected in their search for them not to spot me. You being passed out got their attention enough for it to allow me to sneak away from them."

"This is too much," she thought.

She took off the necklace and through it at the wall on the other side of the room, and she then picked up her phone. She pushed buttons to find out how much money was in her bank account. She stood with a slack jaw in awe. It dumbfounded her even more. So, she searched for and found the necklace, deciding to wear it after all.

"Why are you doing this to me?" she asked in thought after putting the necklace back on.

"I need your help to live here on Earth."

"Why me?" she asked demandingly.

"Your actions showed me you have a trustworthy attitude with fewer complicated obstacles other humans usually have."

"I don't want to help you, not after you just destroyed the career of a star football player."

"I will get him out of his trouble only if you help me with my needs."

"That's extortion. Has he been helping you?"

"I sold him the earrings. He gave them to you before I could listen to his thoughts to determine if he would be willing to help me."

"You have to get him out of trouble before I help you. Didn't you just tell me I'm trustworthy? I promise to help you only if you first help him. Don't you get it? You need to be trustworthy for me to be trustworthy."

"I understand what you want me to do. You are only willing to help me with something that can be bargained as agreeable instead of being extortion. What do you want me to do?"

"Obviously, you and that guy were working together. Do it again. Jump back into the river but wear a life preserver if you really need it."

"When do you want me to do it?"

She stared with an open mouth, surprised by his willing to do what she had just asked of him. She had not expected to have a little control of the situation. She suddenly had a little hope of overcoming it.

"Be on the bridge about noon," she told him. I'll have the earrings on until then. I'm going to try to contact the coach and have him call the police just before you jump. I'm sorry, but they need to know you're still alive. Your situation is your doing, not mine."

"I understand the police are my problem and not your problem. I will again jump off the bike bride if you do what you say you are going to do, and if you do not have the police nearby spying on the situation."

"I will and won't," she thought while on her way to the living room.

"Bard is innocent and I'm going to prove it," she told Donald.

"Why was he on the bridge and able to toss the guy into the river? He was taken into custody and is now likely off the team for good."

"I believe the alien stranger was using him to now be able to use me, but I'm also going to use him, the alien stranger."

"Bard being used is motive for him doing it," Donald rationalized, "especially if he had been given drugs. I hope both of you haven't been doing them, but obviously something has been going on that I'm not being informed of."

"Why would he be doing drugs?"

"Maybe Bard became addictive overcoming an injury," Donald suggested. "He could've got drugs from the guy and was being blackmailed. He could've felt the need to silence him as his only way of getting out of the mess."

"I haven't been doing them," Kayla replied.

"Maybe they were given to you without you knowing it. Maybe Bard had just found out and was upset about it, and just wanted to protect you."

"There's something I haven't told you about. It's a secret. Promise me you'll keep it as such."

"I promise," Donald said shrugging just before leaning forward. "True or not, I'm keeping it to myself."

"The alien stranger has a hummingbird spy. Those earrings detect my thoughts, and he can also communicate back with thought by way of the necklace. I know it's true. I was led by the drone to where he was under a log in the river, and he just channeled our thoughts in the bedroom."

"Do you really believe that?" Donald replied shaking his head. "Drugs make more sense."

"Why would someone like the alien stranger have such advanced technology using it only to sell drugs?" she asked eying the ceiling.

"You should've called the police."

"See you later," she replied walking away.

7
PROVING INNOCENCE

Kayla rode her bicycle to Autzen Stadium in hope of finding the football coach there in his office. She spotted Bard slowly walking across the street towards the bike path. She made it to the other side just before he did in order to get whatever information she could from him. "I'm sure glad you're okay," he said facing her in awe of a fixed gaze.

"My mother's uncle believes you tossed that guy into the river. Was he selling drugs for you wanting to get even?"

"No," he bellowed shaking his frowning face. "I didn't toss him. He jumped. I'm glad to see that you're okay. I was worried about you and baffled as to how you got into the river."

"Is that high a jump possible?"

"It shouldn't be, not even without me holding him. He nearly took me with him."

"How could he have jumped that high?"

"All I know is that I'm in big trouble. I'm indefinitely suspended from the team and being investigated for possible homicide. I'm now out on bail."

"I believe you, but I don't know what to say for now that'll help. I need more information to figure it out. I'm sure you'll be proven innocent and be back on the team once I do."

Bard shrugged eying the sky

"The police seem to think we could be part of a drug ring," he informed her, "and that we wanted to keep him from talking. I could be charged with homicide after they find the body. You could be charged as an accessory just because of me giving you those earrings. It's my fault. I'm sorry for getting you involved."

He gazed at her.

"I see you now have a diamond necklace," he added.

"It's part of the mess we're in," she replied with a few nods.

"How involved are you? What do you know? Why were you in the river?"

"They should've found his body by now if he died," she replied shaking her head, "but they haven't. I believe he's still alive."

"There's no way he could've survived in that current of cold water, especially after falling as far down as he did."

"It's well known people have come back to life from near death."

"That's true," Bard agreed.

"But how did he leap so high?" Kayla asked to be sure of Bard not being more involved.

"I didn't throw him," Bard raised his voice in anger. "Nobody is strong enough to throw that much weight that high."

"Maybe they can if they're on drugs."

"I don't do drugs," he blurted out, "I didn't toss him in the river."

"Maybe he was doing them," she suggested. "Do you know if he was selling them?"

"I just know I bought those earrings from him. I shouldn't have giving them to you. I'm sorry. That was immature of me. You're now wearing a necklace. Why's that?"

"It's too complicated to explain right now. It was nice of you to give me the earrings. Don't be sorry. I believe we're being used. Both of us are innocent and I'm going to prove it."

"That sounds good," he said shaking his head in doubt. "Please, will you inform my lawyer of all you know about it? He needs to prove my innocence for me to turn pro and not go to jail."

She nodded.

"I'm going to do a lot more than that," she said to herself as Bard continued with his slow walk towards the bike path.

She circled around the football stadium and located the office of Coach Molten. She barged into the room and walked up to his desk without any bother to knock and ask for permission to enter.

"I can prove Bard didn't toss that guy into the river," she said to the coach facing her with a curious stare. "He jumped."

Coach Molten shook his head no.

"Nobody throws that much weight that high in the air," Kayla insisted. "He jumped.

"Bard lifts weights," the coach replied. "It's far too high for most anyone to lift, but no one jumps that high."

"Maybe the jumper isn't just anyone."

The coach rubbed his chin staring at Kayla.

"Who are you?" he asked.

"I'm Kayla Chalet, Bard's friend. Maybe he jumped and Bard just assisted him."

"It could've been an accident," the coach conceded, "but Bard's still a part of it."

She leaned forward to stare straight at him.

"He jumped," she insisted, "and he'll do it again."

"Why do you believe he's still alive?" coach Molten asked with a crinkled nose.

"There's no evidence he isn't, and I'll soon have evidence to prove he's alive and well."

"He'll eventually be found by someone," the coach replied shaking his head no, "and most likely deceased."

"I guess you don't want your All American cleared. What kind of coach are you, one that just looks out for his job and not his players?"

He grimaced, facing away from Kayla.

"How can you prove his innocence? I think you just want him to be innocent. Have you two been seeing a lot of each other?"

"We just met. If you take me to the bridge and bring your phone, you'll be able to record what you see for the police to have evidence of Bard's innocence."

"That's it?"

"Trust me. You'll soon find out when we get there."

"Okay, I have some time to spare. Let's go."

He stood up, pointed at the door and picked up his cell phone. He escorted her to his car. She pointed out where they needed to go. It was to circle around by way of driving west to Coburg road, driving south on it until it merged with Franklin Boulevard heading east to where they turned left to take the back road to the bike bridge. As Kayla expected, a hummingbird was hovering nearby the bridge.

"Now what?" the coach asked.

"Get Detective Bentley on the phone," she replied. "We need her to witness this."

The coach pushed buttons on his cell phone.

"Detective Bentley," the coach Molten soon said, "I'm here near the bike bridge from which the guy went into the river. Kayla Chalet claims she has something for us to see that'll prove Bard's innocence."

He pointed his phone at Kayla.

"Do you have visual access to my phone?" he then asked the detective.

Coach Molten nodded yes to Kayla.

Kayla pointed to the cell phone and then at the bike bridge. Coach Molten pointed his cell phone at it.

"We're ready," Kayla thought. "It's time for you to do your thing. If you read my mind, you should know it's not a trap."

What appeared to be a man with long hair took off his wig and leaped about twenty feet above the railing only to dive down into the river. The coach ran to the river, pointing the phone west for sight downstream.

"Did you see that?" the coach shouted with the phone close to his mouth.

Kayla waved her hand, signaling the coach to come forward. She held out her hand to receive the phone.

"This is Kayla," she said holding the phone. "That was the same guy that jumped earlier. He belongs to a secret society having advanced technology. He jumped. Bard is innocent."

"What's going on?" the detective asked.

"Do you think the coach would be part of a hoax? Just show the witnesses of the previous jump what your phone just recorded."

"He needs Bard on the team," the detective replied. "It better not be some kind of hoax."

Kayla handed the phone back to the coach. "I'm now a target, off limits to Bard, don't you think?"

He nodded with a puzzling look on his face.

"I'm going to file a restraining order against you and the whole team as well. That guy who jumped belongs to a secret society. He's using me, and he could use Bard and anybody I befriend."

"Wasn't it dangerous to jump into the river?"

"I'm sure he wore a life preserver and didn't turn himself off like he did the last time."

The coach tilted his head with a crinkled jaw as he eyed the sky. He shook his head pointing at the car.

"I thank you very much Miss Kayla Chalet," he said when they arrived back at Autzen Stadium. "If I can help you in any way, just let me know."

"Is Bard back on the team?"

"It's under consideration."

"What's the problem?"

"I need to know for sure he's hasn't gotten involved with something like drug dealers."

"I'm sure he passed a lie detector and drug test, and is no more than an innocent bystander."

8
STRANGE BANKING

"The guy jumped," Kayla told Donald. "Bard is innocent. I proved it."

"How'd you do that?" Donald asked shaking his head with his eyebrows raised in disbelief.

"I just asked him to jump again."

"Why would he do it?" Donald asked followed by a fixed gaze and open mouth.

"He wants to use me, and I told him I'd only let him do it if he got Bard out of the trouble he'd gotten him into."

"This doesn't make any sense. How does he plan on using you in a way that he has to risk his life?"

"I don't know. He added fifty grand to my checking account."

Donald grimaced while slapping his hand onto his forehead.

"How do you know?" he loudly asked.

"I checked my account online."

"Your purse and phone were returned. He's obviously a hacker. You should go to the police and tell them everything."

"Sorry. I made a promise, and I'm keeping it. You also made a promise, and I need you to keep it as well."

"Okay, if you want to go to jail, that's your choice. I'm completely out of it. Good luck."

"I'm still negotiating. I'll try to spend money to ensure it's really in my account, and he still needs to ensure me I'm not breaking the law."

"You don't hear a word I say, and neither do I hear a word you say."

"Thanks for taking care of me. Maybe I'll be able to use the money for mom's operation."

"You might have to pay your lawyer with it if it's actually in your account and not confiscated as evidence for illegal activity."

Kayla stood in a moment of doubt before going back to her bedroom.

"Where can we soon meet?" she thought to ask after putting the necklace on.

"We can meet to talk in person anytime you want. You only need to go to Alton Baker Park where there are tables with benches to sit on. If you are wearing the earrings, the drone will alert me of your presence and the privacy situation of the surrounding area."

Kayla was soon on her bicycle expecting to meet up with the alien stranger, but only after attempting to use her debit card. She detoured to an electric bicycle shop on Coburg road.

She entered the store and walked around to check out the prices. She pointed at one with a price tag of almost fifteen grand.

"I'll take it," she said to the clerk.

She walked up to the counter and handed the clerk her debit card. He tried processing it on the register. He shook his head after several failures and, with a frowning face and raised eyebrows, handed the debit card back to her.

"Sorry," Kayla apologized. "I guess I need to transfer from my savings. That's a nice bicycle. I'll soon be back for it."

He nodded still appearing suspicious as she turned around to continue on her way to Alton Baker Park to still meet up with the alien stranger.

She recognized Wanda Sue and Jack sitting at a table when she arrived at the park. Kayla peddled up to the table.

"How come you got Bard into trouble?" Wanda Sue asked with an angry appearing stare.

Kayla rubbed the back of her neck while eying ducks swimming on the nearby pond.

"I don't know much about the guy going into the river, or of any connection he had with Bard other than the earrings Bard had given to me. He said he bought them from that guy. That guy also saved me from another guy trying to rape me. He then gave me this necklace to sell for him."

"That guy gave you a necklace," Wanda Sue noted. "Was he your lover? Was his confrontation with Bard that of jealousy and you wanting to get even by telling the police something you preferred they'd believe?"

"No! The guy sold the earring to Bard wanting to use him, but Bard gave them to me."

"What's going on?" Wanda Sue asked.

"I need to find out." Kayla replied. "I'm confused just as much as everyone else is."

"Well," Jack said, "the coach is warning us not to get involved with you, but Bard already is. I'm sure he wants to know what's going on. I know he's innocent. The coach hinted he'll be reinstated if cleared before the season starts."

"He will be," Kayla confirmed. "It just needs time for information that's been verified to be clarified. Be patient. Don't jump to conclusion. I'm sure the situation is going to be straitened out with a good outcome."

Kayla stood sadly concerned by Wanda Sue maintaining her angry stare.

"I'm just trying to be in better control of my life. Bard insisted he wanted to be part of it. I didn't mind, but a bad thing happened. I don't know why it did, but it did, and my life purpose is now to overcome it."

"Well, it's going around campus you're big trouble," Wanda Sue accused.

"Well," Kayla replied facing down and away, "I probably shouldn't have been born. At least I'm not a socialist."

"Take care," Wanda Sue said as she turned to walk away with Jack.

"Sorry," Kayla apologized. "I shouldn't have said that. I didn't mean it. Your economics could be very promising."

Kayla felt it was now her against the world, but most of her life had been a struggle. Maybe it had prepared her for the present situation. She felt she needed to stay the course in order to find out how to cope with her life situations. She knew of no other way, life otherwise having no significant purpose. She decided to accept her destination as her own personal path in life. She felt she needed hope. Maybe she would learn from it. Perhaps everything would come out okay, as she wanted to believe, but there was plenty of doubt to consider along with losing would-be-friends she wanted to have.

She noticed the hummingbird hovering near the bike bridge close to the Coburg overpass. She sat down at the table expecting the alien stranger to arrive any moment. She noticed, as well, Bard jogging towards her from the direction of Autzen Stadium.

"Hi!" he greeted her. "The coach told me you're off limits, but there's no need to worry; I'll never hurt you. I'm no longer on the football team, but the coach told me there is evidence that the guy who jumped into the river is alive and well, and that I could be reinstated by the time the season starts."

"Sorry," Kayla apologized. "I'm also in deep trouble with something I didn't want to get you involved with, but you insisted giving me those earrings that some guy tried to take from me. He threatened to rape me before the other guy saved me. The next day I was talking to that guy who saved me when the other one came towards us. He chased my savior with a knife."

"Yeah, I reckon I should have known it pays to help someone I really care about, and I still do. I'm sorry I insisted you take the earrings. I need to be more mature and not so bossy."

"You don't need to be sorry," she said with a shrug. "I shouldn't have worn them while on my way home. How come you're not back on the team? I proved your innocence."

His eyes opened wide.

"You proved my innocence?"

"Yes," she replied nodding. "I found the guy that jumped. I got him to confess, and he even showed your coach and the police how he did it. He even jumped back into the river."

Bard stared at her in disbelief.

"Well, I'm thankful for that, but the rumor going around is that they found a bomb on him, and I'm now a hero. The Fed is investigating. They asked me about you. They seem to believe we played around with a leaping gadget to fool them and not get caught for drug trafficking. Is the dude a drug dealer or something worse?"

As she shrugged, she saw the alien stranger a good distance away approaching them.

"He's coming," she said pointing at the alien stranger. "We might be about to find out. You'll just need to stay and listen."

When the alien stranger came close enough to be recognized, Bard gazed with open mouth at him, appearing a lot more astonished than Coach Molten had been when he had witnessed the leap off the bridge.

"I am not a terrorist," the alien stranger informed when finally arriving close enough for a personal conversation. "I did not have a bomb, and I do not traffic drugs."

"You're alive," Bard said with a bewildering look on his face. "Who saved you?"

"Kayla Chalet saved me."

"How'd she do that? How did you hear what we said, and how can you jump so high?"

"I belong to a secret society. We are scientists with more advanced knowledge than other scientists have so far learned of."

"Why are the Feds after you?"

"They are probably alarmed by my ability to leap as high as I did to dive into the river and survive, and they are probably also concerned with my having expensive jewelry to sell. They could suspect that I am a threat to the nation, but I have no intention to take it over or to do any harm to it."

"Don't you?" Kayla asked. "Why are you using me? Why does my bank account now show more than fifty grand in it that I'm unable to use? I reckon I'm in trouble with the law instead of you being in trouble with it."

Bard stood gazing back-and-forth at Kayla and the alien stranger as they spoke.

"The fifty grand is for you to purchase anything you want to have for special needs."

"I tried to spend it. It was rejected."

"I apologize to you for not having activated it yet into your actual account."

"Why's that?"

"I am allowing you to decide if you want to accept the responsibility of spending the money."

"So, I'm not in any danger until I spend the money. Is there anyway someone can trace it back to me?"

"Your account is only detectable online during the time you use it to transfer its monetary value to another account. The choice of using it is yours to make."

"It'd be nice to have the money, but not if it sends me to prison."

"The authorities will only be able to detect the transactions you make whenever you make them, but you will still be able to claim money that is in your account is an anomalous donation you know nothing about."

"How will I be able to sleep at night by not knowing if I'm spending stolen money?"

"If you use the money for a generous purpose, you will sleep peacefully at night and feel better about your purpose in life."

"I guess it is stolen since you're not denying it."

"I am stealing it from criminals selling drugs to addictive customers."

"That makes it dangerous. Is it worth dying for?"

"It could be worth living for."

"What do you consider to be generous?"

"I consider helping the homeless for them to have better conditions to live in, and for them to be either cured of or prevented from having drug addiction, is a generous endeavor. Helping to create a social environment of real wealth of valuable products instead of just a monetary competition of wealth, and helping counter the grave effects of climate change for creating a more livable environment are other generous endeavors."

"That's a tall order."

"The choice is yours to make. I am here to provide the means of success for your willingness to help me help others, but you will need to apply your own capability as well."

"If I donate stolen money, I'm still a thief in the eyes of the law, and I'll have to confess to the police and tell them all I know about you."

"If you transfer the money back into the account you received it from, then you will only be a participant in the transaction without having knowledge of its origin. Without knowing of it being stolen, it is not against the law for just participating in something that is considered to be a good cause."

"Why does it need to be in my account?"

"You will then be responsible for whatever it is spent on."

"So, I'm in charge of someone. Who is it?"

"You will be charge of the actual spender."

"Who is it?"

"He is the fellow that was lying on the bike path the other night."

"This is getting crazier and crazier."

She eyed Bard shaking his head and turning to walk away. She followed him a little ways.

"Do you believe that guy?" he asked.

"I need to think about it."

"You might be putting yourself in danger."

"Yeah, I might be putting you and others in danger as well, but what else can I do? I need to sleep at night and won't be able to without knowing where I stand."

"My lawyer could help you figure that out."

She eyed Bard.

"I'd like that. I'm going to talk to your lawyer if he really wants me to?"

"I'll let him know he does. He only gets paid if he proves my innocence."

"Actually, it's already been proven."

"That guy seems like a con. He's probably got a listening device to spy on people and to use their words to his advantage. Did he really give you all that money?"

"I don't know. I wasn't able to spend it. He might or might not be telling the truth."

Bard frowned shaking his head no.

"He's the proof himself," she noted.

"He's also a computer nerd and hacker for sure," Bard accused, "and he seems to have additional capabilities with the possibility of taking over control of anything or anyone he wants to."

Kayla stopped. He faced her. She pointed at an earring while crossing her lips with another finger.

He shrugged. She shrugged.

"Part of the listening device is the earrings. He also has a spy drone disguised as a hummingbird. It appears that secret society of advance knowledge is a credible possibility. Now, he knows you know. I reckon he trusts you as well as me. Seal your lips to just wait and see."

Bard faced the ground with a crinkled nose shaking his head in disbelief, but he then nodded eying Kayla.

"I'm never giving anyone else diamond earrings from now on. The guilt is worse than the pain."

"I don't blame you for giving them to me. You didn't know his intent, and you intended to do the right thing. Don't feel guilty for something someone else did. That'll just let them be in control of your life."

"That's excellent advice. I'll see you soon at the restaurant."

"I was laid off, and your life and career will be at risk if we continue to see each other."

"No!" Bard said slapping his forehead. "Hey, Wanda Sue said they might add a pool table to the dining room. We still have the commitment to that social club. I hope to see you there."

"I don't think the owner wants me there."

"He wanted me there, and I'm sure he still does. I just need your phone number to invite you."

She gave him her phone number. He waved goodbye and turned to walk away. She walked back to the table.

"You must know what I told Bard."

"I do and I am okay with it."

"I really don't understand why you need to use me. You seem to have all the capability to achieve anything you want to."

"It is still too risky for just me to do without help with someone as trustworthy as you are."

"You have a lot of knowledge that could buy the silence of anyone wanting the money."

"That would be unlawful of me."

"You've been using me."

"You are almost correct. I used human DNA to grow this body, but its nutritional needs are complex. Your understanding of them seems to be better than most all other humans. I need it more than just your silence."

"So, you're not from this planet. I suspected that."

"You also have more of an open mind than most other humans. My health also depends on a healthy climate. Your associate Wanda Sue is knowledgeable of a climate change threat that has economic consequences. Your participation in that social group is needed for me to help in its remedy. I agree with your informing Bard of what you know of me, and I am willing to use my advanced technology to protect him and all others you associate with."

"I sure hope you're not just leading us on."

"I just intend to provide a means for you to lead yourself to a more purposeful lifestyle."

"Why'd you plot that trap on the bike path?"

"It was not plotted. The guy had heartburn and was frustrated. He had taken more drugs. It became evident I wasn't able to trust him. I no longer gave him access to his bank account. He became angry of its consequence, and he had gotten heartburn. You became his victim. I rescued you for both of your concerns. I have learned more about you because of you wearing the earrings, and I believed you to be sincere and trustworthy by way of your response. I now feel indebted to you."

"Can't that other guy buy what you need?"

"I can only trust him with a limited amount of capital, and I prefer to use his bank account only to transfer to your bank account. That will identify him as the original receptive of capital income needed for my needs. It becomes charity to you to also give as charity, but as charity for a greater purpose in life."

"Well, it now seems to be do-it-or-lose-it, but it is stolen money."

"It is stolen money donated to you that you will donate back for a better purpose to the account your account received it from."

She gazed at the sky as he walked away. It was a risky involvement in something she had little knowledge of, but she had need of more income, and she wanted to have more purpose in life. Having significant control of how it can be spent might be a capable path to achieve it. However, she also had concerns of Bard being involved. She had a crush on him, but felt she needed to avoid him in being responsible for his safety.

9
BECOMING A SPY

Kayla entered the office wearing neither the necklace nor the earrings.

"Hi," Kayla said to the guy sitting at a desk. "Bard Sucrets said you wanted to talk to me."

"Are you Kayla Chalet?"

"Yes, I am."

"Have a seat. I'd like to know all you know."

"Bard said the police suspect we're part of a secret society," she replied while sitting down in front of the desk.

"Are you?" the lawyer asked.

"Bard gave me earring he bought from the guy who jumped into the river, and who was peddling them. I also had a confrontation with the guy who had chased the jumper to the bridge. The jumper had rescued me from him the night before, so it seemed at the time, and he then gave me a necklace to sell for him. He put money in my bank account claiming it was a donation. That's all I know. It appears I'm being used. I'm not sure if there's anything I can do about it."

"If the money is donated," he said, "it could be legal, but you need to report it as taxable income, and you could be an accessory to criminal activity if it's stolen."

Kayla bowed rubbing her forehead.

"What if the money is not actually in my account; I'm only using it as a charity donation from another account? That's what the jumper claims we're doing, me being in control of the account I give it back to."

"If it's from a criminal organization, you can be prosecuted as an accessory. You could be convicted even if the donor is anonymous. If you only transfer it from one account to another, then you are still a participant."

"What should I do?"

"You should go to the authorities and report it. With your cooperation they would then have no reason to charge you with any criminal activity, and they would have a different direction to follow for their investigation."

"Thanks. Is it okay for me to pay you from my bank account?"

"No. There's no charge. I'm following up on another investigation. It involves you with Bard. You're part of his expense, but not if you need me to defend you in court."

"I've been his expense from the moment of first meeting him," she replied facing the floor with a frowning face.

"You said the guy jumped and is using you. That was in the present tense."

"He did jump, and he did it again yesterday. The football coach and the detective both witnessed it."

He gazed at her.

"I know it's hard to believe," she said with a shrug. "I'm sure his coach will confirm it if you give him a call."

"I surely will," he agreed.

"Thanks for the advice," she said. "I appreciate it and will follow through on it."

He nodded.

She left somewhat encouraged with the advice given to her, believing she finally had a way of being in control of her life by confronting the destiny of which she otherwise had little if no control whatsoever.

She rode her bicycle straight to the police station to discuss her situation with the police. The clerk directed her to the office of Detective Bentley. A tall slim man was also in the room.

"She's Kayla Chalet," Detective Bentley said facing the tall slim fellow.

"I'm a federal agent," the tall slim fellow introduced himself. "What has occurred of late is very unusual with possible consequence. A thorough investigation is warranted."

"I took a lie detector."

"I examined it. Bard Sucrets also took one, and we now know someone has been peddling expensive jewelry. The police have arrested a guy fitting the description of the guy who had chased the peddler. They searched him to find these diamond earrings in his pocket. The diamonds are commercially made, but appear real and likely expensive. If you confirm they were stolen from you, they'll be kept here for being evidence, and you could get them back if he's found guilty and you're innocent."

"Sorry. They're not mine. I somehow found my stuff when I got home from the hospital."

"Really," the agent seemed to ask.

"Did you hear the statement I made when I took the lie detector?" Kayla asked.

"I did," the agent confirmed. "Even though those diamonds are commercially made, we've haven't found any transmitters in them. I also looked at that second jump off the bridge. Your story appears confirmable, but we have no evidence of any hacking into your bank account. Still, your claim of a secret society is now considered likely. Your reporting it is sincerely appreciated."

"Bard's lawyer advised me I could be prosecuted as an accessory to illegal activity unless I go to the police. That's why I'm here; to make sure I'm not breaking the law."

"So far we know of no actual law violations, but we do need to know more about this secret society."

"Is that itself a crime?"

"No, it's not, but being an illegal alien and a spy justifies our investigation for already being criminal activity. If that secret society has advanced technology, it could be a threat to the welfare of our nation. We might need your help to discover its intent."

"Are you asking me to be a spy?"

"We can sure use your help. Don't you want to serve your nation?""

"I'll help only if it's not undercover."

"A spy is undercover."

"There's a problem," she said with a shrug.

"What is it?" he asked staring attentively at her.

"I'll need to inform the alien stranger what I'm up to."

"Why's that?" he asked still maintaining his attentive stare.

"He reads my mind. He'll know I contacted you if he doesn't already by now. If I don't inform him why I'm here, he'll likely not trust me with anything that could expose him."

"That's a good point," he replied shaking his head as if in disbelief, "but we still need you to keep us informed. If he asks you to do something against the law, we'll know you are innocent if you inform us of what they plan to do."

"It's certain I don't want to break the law," she answered with a stare. "That's why I'm here telling you it's what it is, such that neither he nor you have any reason to use me."

"We need your help, Miss Kayla Chalet. The welfare of the nation could be at stake."

She paused.

"You won't prosecute me if I do what I'll be asked to do even if it breaks the law?"

"As long as you keep us informed, you will not be prosecuted for it."

"What if I'm unable to inform you?"

"It'll be considered as a necessity, but that consideration further includes the possibility of using our trust against us. I'm sorry, it's conditional. That's how it has to be."

"I understand there are no guarantees," she said with a pause, "but it'll be more difficult to live in a destroyed nation. I'm patriotic. I'll do my best to keep you informed."

"Thank you, Miss Kayla Chalet."

"How do I contact you to inform you?"

"Detective Bentley is in charge of you here. You just report directly to her. Okay?"

"Okay."

As the agent left the room, Detective Bentley stood up from her chair and handed Kayla a photo.

"Do you recognize him?"

"He's the one who chased the alien stranger onto the bridge. He sort of tried to rape me the night before."

She did recognize the long hair and raggedy beard. It indicated the law already knew more about the secret society than they were letting on.

"We've taken him into custody for suspicion of robbery. He was peddling the earrings you now have in your possession. Are you positive they aren't yours?"

"They're just the same. I left mine at home."

"Well, I guess all we have against him is attempted rape, but he's the only member of the secret society we have other than you. Are you willing to cooperate?"

"Yeah, I believe for sure he and the alien stranger set me up."

"We could add a charge of attempted rape."

"Don't tell me you want me to use him to get what you want?" Kayla asked crossing her arms tight against her chest. She firmly stared at Detective Bentley because of not being comfortable of spying on someone who had threatened her.

It was only a momentary reaction. After all, he was also the guy she was to be in charge of his spending of stolen money. She had become the police instead of having to call them.

"He's the only lead we now have," Detective Bentley continued to inform. "He had been arrested before for possession of drugs, but he had also been a talented basketball player before being injured. He became addicted taking opioids. Hopefully we'll be able to bargain with him for his cooperation."

Kayla rubbed her head behind her ear while considering what was appropriate to do. Would it either be complying with the law now wanting her to use the guy who attempted to rape her, or would it be in total compliance with the alien stranger having her in charge of spending stolen money. Perhaps she could do both for a better overall result.

"The alien stranger did tell me I should help provide for the homeless and to help confront global warming. I could play along with it, but I'll need a lot of help and protection from those drug cartels coming after us."

"What's your plan," the detective asked.

Kayla paused to think up a possible solution to the situation. She reached for her cell phone and accessed her checking account. She gazed with a slack jaw seeing more than two hundred thousand dollars in it.

"This guy has a banking account. The alien stranger claims to use it to transfer money to my account. I need to find out if I was told the truth, and that the money is in my account as indicated. I'll try to transfer some back into the other account, but the alien stranger might not activate my account if he's aware of me being here. I need to try. Is that okay?"

"It's a good idea, but it's to be between you and the person with the other account."

Kayla attached the earrings to her ears.

"Why did you put the earrings on? You said they aren't yours."

"As I claimed, the alien stranger uses them to hear what I say. It lets him know I want to transfer money from my account to this guy's account. When can I ask him?"

Detective Bentley pushed a speaker button.

"Please escort the prisoner to my office."

She faced Kayla.

"He'll be here any minute; just be patient."

"Have you noticed a hummingbird hovering somewhere nearby here lately?" Kayla asked.

She grinned, eying Kayla.

Kayla pointed a finger at the earrings, but then shook her head no.

"I'm a bird watcher," Kayla fibbed realizing the alien stranger could be counter spying now that she was wearing the earrings.

The detective eyed the ceiling.

The guy that Kayla had encountered along with the alien stranger entered the room along with a policeman. The policeman left after the guy sat down beside Kayla.

She barely was able to scoot her chair a few inches away from him. His presence countered the presence of lawful authorities.

"As you must know," Detective Bentley said staring at the prisoner, "we can add attempted rape and murder, but your victim is right here. She told me she wants to make a deal for you to help us discover and prevent the going on of a more hideous crime."

The prisoner eyed Kayla.

"I'll forgive you," she claimed.

"I'm sorry for what I did," he apologized. "I wasn't myself."

"Who are you?"

"I'm a homeless victim of circumstance."

"What's your name?"

"They didn't tell you I'm James Baker?"

"How many girls have you rapped?"

"None," he blurted out. "I've just been confused. Growing up I was subjected to Playboy and all kinds of stuff in movies. The heroes got the girls by being more aggressive. Some girls were mad at me for not chasing them; others became offended by it. I feared both rejection and commitment. Both my dad and mom had jobs, and they went out drinking after work for me to grow up a loaner trying to figure it out."

"How do you relate with the alien stranger? Don't you work for him?"

"He helped me overcome my addiction and has provided a place for me to stay. He helped me and I now help him, but I can only do what I can, and he doesn't trust me anymore."

"Are you selling drugs?"

"No," he replied, "not now."

"But you did sell them."

"I did, but only to survive. You know who stopped me. I no longer need to do it."

"Does the alien stranger sell them?"

"No, he just helped me stop doing it, but he knows who sells them and is able to use them and protect me at the same time."

"Would he protect me if I helped you?"

"I'm sure he would. How can you help me?"

"What do you need?"

"I need money."

"Do you have access to your bank account?"

"I sure do, even though I no longer have an address. It's online, but I can use my debit card or write checks if they're allowed, as he somehow has a way of hiding it from use."

"Can I add twenty thousand to it?"

"Who do I have to kill?" he asked with narrow eyed expression. "What's the catch?"

"You'll need to donate for a good cause. A social club recently formed at an inn. You need to buy whatever clothes you need to appear as a wealthy donor, and you'll need to cooperate with the police to bring drug dealers to justice."

"If only I could and did rat on any of those guys, I'd be dead in no time, and they'd surely find out what I'm doing."

"Don't you want more control of your life?" Detective Bentley asked.

"Okay, put money in my bank account and I'll give it a go," James replied while staring at the floor. "So what if I'm killed? What's the big deal?"

"The donor can be anonymous," Kayla said. "You'll just need to let me be in control of your account."

"Why's that?"

"The alien stranger is putting me in charge."

"What?" James blurted out.

"I reckon it's to allow me to stay undercover. You'll be up front to do the transactions. I'm just to make sure you'll do what you're supposed to, and there's another condition."

"What that?" he asked with twisted lips.

"My mother has cancer and is in need of an expensive operation. I need you to donate one hundred thousand to the hospital to cover it."

He shrugged and slapped his head.

"You know who can make it happen?" Kayla assured him. "He needs to allow it for him to have my help."

"Do I get to spend any of it?" James asked.

"Yes. I'll make sure you get what you need if it's not heroin or something like that, and I'm sure the alien stranger is going to protect both of us."

He nodded seemingly approving what Kayla had told him while the police detective continued to shake her head while sitting.

Kayla eyed her phone wondering if the alien stranger was listening in and willing to transfer the money from her account. The transfer appeared to occur after only a few minutes, and appeared to decrease after about another minute.

Did it really occur? Did the alien stranger reactivate her account as he had promised?

She disconnected from her account to then hand the phone to James.

"Was a hundred and twenty grand added to your account?" she asked.

He nodded after connecting to it.

"Okay, let's call the hospital to donate that hundred grand."

They called the hospital and James was able to make a hundred-grand-transfer with the hospital's confirmation of it.

The police now had evidence of her having an unknown source of capital. Being from foreign banks of an unknown source, it likely connected with drug trafficking. She had become entangled amongst criminal activity, the secret society and the law, but hopefully no one other than the law would be able to trace it back to her account.

At least she had learned James Baker had proper identification and was willing to put his life in danger by accepting stolen money. She also had a plan that involved bringing into the mix Bard, Wanda Sue, and Jack. However, that involvement of others, especially of Bard, placed a lot more responsibility on her shoulders.

10
REAL WEALTH ECONOMICS

Kayla entered the diner when Wanda Sue was clearing a table. Kayla took a seat at another table. Wanda Sue shrugged as she left with the remaining used dishes.

"What's up?" Wanda Sue asked when she came back.

"I have a proposal," Kayla replied with the palm of her hand facing up beside her shoulder.

"I'd like to hear it," Wanda Sue replied as she sat down on the other side of the table. "I heard from Jack that you helped prove Bard's innocence."

"Yes, I did," Kayla said leaning slightly forward and eying Wanda Sue, "and my proposal has to do with Mr. Olsen's proposal of that social group. I know someone who wants to donate a lot of money for a good cause, like climate change."

"That sounds good."

"It involves hiring potential owners, and it's about creating more ownership of businesses, which becomes another enterprise in itself."

"That's quite an ambitious proposal, but unfortunately I'm tied up with this place. It needs my full attention, and your joint venture needs trusted individuals beyond yourself."

"It won't just be me. I'll have the donor and others to help out as well, and the social club could make it happen. You know the economics and Jack is a physicist and biochemist. We just need to come up with some innovative ideas, such as remedies for curing addictions of the homeless. It could put drug traffickers out of business."

"Who's the donor?" Wanda Sue asked with a creased brow.

"He insists on remaining anonymous, wanting to be a Secret Santa."

"How do you know he's trustworthy and will do what he claims?" Wanda Sue asked eying the ceiling.

"My mother has cancer in need of expensive surgery. He donated a hundred grand, and he can do a lot more with a good accountant. You'll be paid for it."

"Really," Wanda Sue replied with raised eyebrows.

"It's real, and it's on your free time helping with such transactions as buying RV's, property in eastern Oregon, trucks and so forth. All of it will be charity to potential home owners willing to combat climate change."

"Well, it'll be less boring than this place. Let's discuss some economics regarding how government affects it."

"How can we prevent and get out of the next recession?" Kayla asked with a shrug.

"They need to raise the debt ceiling instead of just raising taxes."

"Wouldn't that result in rapid inflation?" Kayla asked with another shrug.

"That's jus conservative politics of the rich not wanting change to occur that could benefit the poor more than them. A major problem with our free enterprise system is monopoly or oligopoly. If the rich gain way too much of an advantage, the American dream becomes just a dream."

"Doesn't money grow on trees?" Kayla asked with a grin and a shrug.

"Money isn't real wealth. What it can buy is what determines it value. Products are true wealth."

"Doesn't money allow us free choice to buy what we want?"

"Inflation usually results with not enough products to satisfy more demand. Just before becoming a nation we just kept printing more money. It became worthless, but France considered our credit rating higher than England's."

"Well, they were England's competitors, weren't they?"

"Yeah, but we were part of the competition. We had lots of land potential to develop. They wanted part of it, and that's what credit is all about."

"Still, didn't you say inflation made our money worthless?"

"I did, but it was a step in the right direction. It needs to be done right. If increasing the debt ceiling or more credit allows for both more production and its purchase, then it balances out for no need of inflation to occur."

"Doesn't someone like our grandchildren have to pay off the debt?"

"No," Wanda Sue clamored. "That's political nonsense. Leaving roads, bridges and so forth to fix is debt left for our grandchildren. If we own the national debt that we create, there's no need to pay it back to ourselves. It's just credit allowing us to do more. To plant crops for food, you need to prepare the land. Credit helps to allow it."

"You still have to pay it back, don't you?" Kayla insisted to ask.

"Yes, you do," Wanda Sue somewhat agreed. "Government sees the potential value of the land allowing it to happen. If it doesn't, then it'll get the land and sell it to someone else. Food is needed. If farmers don't raise the crops to pay back the loan, then they likely lose. But, food is needed. Government could also invest in ways to help make land more fertile. However, I also admit, the greater amount of growers as more competition can end up with individual cost of production higher than profit. Food stamps could be needed to increase demand."

Kayla shook her head facing the table.

"There can be negative results," Wanda Sue admitted. "It's a matter of doing it right. If done right, it'll work. If done wrong, then it won't work. Still, inflation occurs because of more demand what the cost of production allows."

"Doesn't money just grow on trees?" Kayla reiterated with a stare.

"Money is a facilitator," Wanda Sue continued to explain. "If one dollar moves fast enough, it could buy everything. A credit card more easily allows that to happen. There's no need for trees or anything like gold."

"Didn't gold provide a common currency for all nations?"

"We along with France obtained three-fourth of all the available gold. Along came the Great Depression. It occurred mostly with nations on the gold standard. Those that temporary got off it recovered sooner. We were last to get off and last to recover. Nixon finally got us off it for good."

"So, should we no longer use paper money as well?"

"The real problem is with interest rates. They go up and down during times of inflation and deflation. Those of us living on the edge are more likely to fall off. If we can't pay our way out of debt, then bankrupts occur with less accessible demand. On the other hand, those with money to spare have more options. If banks pay lower interest rates to depositors, which can even go down to zero, stocks become a better option when it's realized that recovery is on its way. But, that also decreases monetary credit for the purchase of goods. The rich get richer and the poor get poorer."

"Still," Kayla asked with a crinkled nose, "don't those of us who manage with a better strategy become more successful? Isn't that how you win at pool? Doesn't free competition have positive outcome?"

"That's part of it," Wanda Sue partly conceded. "Microsoft got rich producing a great product, and its owners have shared its wealth with needed projects, but there're other parts as well. Establishment in complete control can also outweigh our freedom to compete. If the rich buy up all the land, then the poor are just that much more in debt. Too much of anything is usually not a good thing. Like Jack said, there are states of equilibrium that are maintained by adjustment. It applies to economics as well."

"What do we need to do in order to adjust?"

"What's the economic value of air?"

"We can't live without it," Kayla said while rubbing her forehead and facing the wall, "but its pollution somehow needs to be cleaned up. I suppose it has a negative economic value for some of us having to pay more for products."

"That would be right with more restrictive credit, and more carbon in the air results in more damage along with more cost of rebuilding. But, if solar energy is used to produce product a lot cleaner as well as cheaper, it's then a positive for the general economy as a whole. Product is a true measure of wealth. Use all that solar energy in the right way to make it and we'll have it."

"Shouldn't people be free to live their lives their own way?"

"Yeah, shouldn't we all be free to go shoot and kill anyone we want?"

"Of course not; we do need law and order in order to get along. What do you propose?"

"If circumstances are too much for a single individual to overcome, then social conformity of combining our efforts becomes a better option for success."

"What do you propose for climate change?"

"Suppose government finances the production of solar charging stations along highways for electric cars, wouldn't that be a positive?"

"Wouldn't more tax be needed to pay for it?"

"They could just raise the debt ceiling, but it could have a negative effect on some of us, like those who produce or buy stocks of fossil fuels."

"Yeah, how's it not going to cost them?"

"There has to be a compromise."

"How can that happen?"

"Government credit for financing the construction of highways is social. It complements free enterprise in being a social capitalism positive, but a social capitalism regarding electric charging stations can be a negative to those more dependent on fossil fuels. But, if government also remedies the fossil fuel loss by allowing it to be part of the transition, then it could be part of the overall positive as well without penalization of past success. We just need to share the positive results."

"In other words," Kayla replied, "we need to buy them out."

"Seven times more water than oil is pulled out of the ground. It just needs to be purified. Free solar energy could do it, and the oil could be used for plastic barrels to hold water for it not to evaporate into the air for more storage of heat."

11
SUMMER LAKE

"I don't know about this," Peter said sitting beside Donald in the backseat of Jack's car on its way to Summer Lake. "I want to live my life, not have someone live it for me. Money should be our freedom to spend on what we want."

"Spending money is spending freedom," Donald replied. "Even though you're free to choose, conforming could be needed to make it happen. You choose who to marry, but she has a choice as well, and conditions of that vow need to be met."

"Owning that property at Summer Lake comes with truck loads of conditions," Peter complained with a sneer. "They say I have to stay there and develop it. That might not be possible."

"He's right," Carl said sitting in the front seat beside Jack, who was behind the wheel, "I'm selling it for that reason. That alkaline soil is extremely difficult to change. On top is ten feet of hard clay with a slight decline towards the lake. Below that is sandy soil hundreds of feet deep. What little water comes along either runs off or sinks too deep down."

"It could be an opportunity to advance your way of life," Donald insisted. "Take it or leave it. It's your choice.

Freedom is only good if you use it. Following a choice often involves a commitment whereby you can earn more of them if you make the right ones to commit to."

"How am I going to do anything by myself" Peter replied shaking his head and gritting his teeth.

"You'll soon be with some of your buddies," Donald informed him. "The donor hired them to help you out."

"Why did you buy the property?" Peter asked Carl.

"I needed to get out of the valley with all that spring and summer pollen," he answered. "I tried it here, but it didn't work. I had to go back and deal with it."

"What did you come up with?" Donald asked.

"I researched the internet and found out that I have all the symptoms of cystic fibrosis. I have thick toenails and no upper body fat. I was unable to gain weight after high school no matter how much I ate. I'm unable to store water. My saliva glands use it to make more saliva. It then plugs up my passage way to the lungs. I tried burping out toxic gas. It helped, but when I fainted with heartburn, and medics told me I was dehydrated, I tried drinking more water. It just got worse. I finally figured out I needed to spit out that saliva before it became snot."

"How'd you get that way?" Peter asked.

"I believe it was because doctors removed my tonsils and appendix. They claimed we didn't need them anymore, but now they only remove part of the tonsils."

"Doctors save lives," Donald said, "and mostly know what they're doing, but that's not always the case. I had a kidney stone that they said was too big to pass on, and that I needed an operation to remove it. But, the narcotic medicine they prescribed for pain didn't work. I didn't eat, but I drank a large Pepsi. The pain soon went away. When I went back for that operation, the x-rays found no kidney stone."

"I had a couple kidney stones," Carl said, "but I now have a more acid diet."

"That could give you ulcers," Donald warned.

"What would be better?" Carl asked.

"I cook my oats in pure cow's milk along with bananas, cinnamon, nutmeg, ginger and sesame seeds. It's a very nutritious diet."

"Why do you include all that?" Peter asked.

"Milk is balanced in vitamins and minerals. The potassium in the bananas balances sodium in milk. Cinnamon synthesizes sugar with muscles for it not to be stored as liver fat. Ginger is good for the digestive system. Nutmeg and sesame seeds have lots of nutritional benefits. Seeds in particular are like nutritional medicine. Life grows from them, but they're difficult to digest. In my mid seventies I became aware I was losing my memory. I came up with Tamari roasted pumpkin seeds. It just happened to be the nutrition my brain was missing. After one tablespoon a day for three weeks, I noticed improvement."

"Have you been able to do anything about your allergies?" Peter asked.

"Being around dogs I got really plugged up. My wife lit a vanilla candle. It all cleared away. I tried sipping a little vanilla. It helped. It seemed to thin the snot allowing it to pass on down, but it also allowed my saliva glands to secrete more saliva. I had to spit a lot more to avoid heartburn."

"So, is it bad or good?" Peter asked with a shrug.

"You need to find the right balance. It can be helpful in the spring and early summer to combat all that pollen, but in the late fall and winter I need less water and no vanilla. The saliva tends to be thicker for me not having to spit out as much."

They had passed by the Ponderosa trees in the Cascades and descended down into a high desert area. With only one last mountainous hill to pass over, they finally closed in towards the north side of the actual lake near the Summer Lake resort,

They turned left off the main road to follow another road. They turned right off the other road to park nearby a truck and an RV.

"There sure isn't much here," Peter noted.

Donald pointed at a couple guys standing beside a truck.

"That's a couple of your buddies that have come to help you get started. They could become your neighbors. You have plenty of food in this RV, and there's an inn and restaurant over by the rock cliff where I'll be staying for a month. Those two guys will also be bringing you whatever you'll need. You need to do the rest."

They got out of the car to join the other guys.

Donald pointed at wind turbines behind the truck. Some were large and some were tiny, all the turbines being three half cylinders spaced evenly apart around a pole to catch the wind from any direction to rotate magnets to, in turn, create an electromagnetic field for generating electricity in a wire to charge batteries.

"To generate electricity," Donald informed, "all you need is to change a magnetic field close to a wire. Those small turbines will catch a breeze. The big ones will catch stiff wind. Those solar panels on top of the RV will also charge batteries. You'll have all the electricity you'll need to power robots or whatever."

Peter shrugged.

A pickup truck entered the lot and parked close to them. In the back of it was a load of brush.

"That's a couple more guys that volunteered to help you get started," Donald informed Peter. "They are also potential buyers."

A guy got out and started unloading wood that he carried over to where another guy had started a campfire.

Jack reached inside a sack and brought out a paper cup and a glass. He held one in one hand and the other in the other hand.

"Should I boil water in this paper cup or in the glass?" he asked standing by the fire that was getting hot from the Mountain Mahogany that burned so hot for it not to smoke.

"Are you serious?" Peter asked.

"Well," Jack replied, "this one might be too hot."

Jack put some other wood on the fire for it to smoke. He then filled both the paper cup and glass with water. He then placed them on top of hot coals within the campfire.

"How can that be?" Peter asked when water began to boil with no change whatsoever of the glass or paper cup.

"It takes a thousand degrees to ignite paper," Jack informed. "Water boils at a hundred and eighty. Heat is kinetic energy that can go through the paper and glass right to the water that absorbs it. However, don't try putting out a grease fire with water; you'll only fuel it, as I did once from cooking eggs in grease. When I tried to put out the fire, it lit my house on fire. I was quick to put it out, but burned my hand doing it."

"Why do I need a campfire anyway?" Peter asked. "Can't I cook in the RV?"

"You can," Jack answered. "The campfire is just to illustrate. Alkaline soil needs to be fertilized. You can turn waste into fertilizer just by heating it apart from air. Seven hundred degrees does the trick. Get too much above that and you'll make charcoal that you don't want. Get hotter and you'll make bombs, but it can also become diamonds with enough pressure to make it happen."

"You can help prevent forest fires," Donald said, "by getting those dead limbs up there to heat into fertilizer, but it's going to take a long time along with tremendous effort. You're just the start of something bigger. More land owners are needed to make it happen."

"There needs to be a way of using that hard clay and sandy soil beneath it," Jack said. "You're going to have to redevelop it in a way it can maintain needed amounts of water for agriculture."

"How do I do that?" Peter asked.

"It's going to take time," Jack warned. "It'll be helpful to build a compost bin within a closure for the bin to leak water in a way it can be reused."

"Why does it need to leak and be reused?"

"Worms can turn shredded paper into fertilizer that's only a little wet. To transform alkali soil into more acid soil it needs nitrogen. Even though air has plenty of it, it's not in a useable form to grow stuff in a garden, but worms can transform it. Your kidneys also flush it out. It's a major ingredient of protein that helps control all that carbon energy of sugar in transforming it into various acids. Water is only good if you don't drown in it."

Peter shrugged.

"Do you know what's in pure sugar besides carbon and hydrogen?" Jack asked.

Peter shrugged again.

"Lots of oxygen," Jack informed. "It can be converted into water. They claim about ninety-five percent of a tomato can be water."

"Isn't water healthy for you?"

"It's about how atoms bond together," Jack answered. "Heating stuff at higher temperature bonds it with more energy. Cook food at moderate temperature for it to be easier to digest. Heat it at a higher temperature and it tends to plug up the joints and digestive system, and even the heart. But, it's reversible. Stop eating too much of stuff like potato chips that are cooked at high temperature, or even eggs cooked in grease."

"Food is essential wealth," Donald said. "We need to produce more in a harmonious way of Earth not heating up. Our healthy bodies maintain a ninety-eight degree temperature for it to maintain its particular state of equilibrium, and Earth also needs to maintain a livable temperature for it to maintain a more desirable state of equilibrium for us to live in."

"What can I grow here?" Peter asked with a shrug.

"Tomatoes are very healthy for the skin and bones," Donald said. "They can even help cure or prevent cancer. Dark raisins or grape skins do likewise, and are good for digestion and the right amount of blood sugar."

"That's good to know," Peter acknowledged.

"However," Jack said, "I hear you're going to have plenty of neighbors. If too much competition lowers the price below the cost of production, it won't work."

"Yeah," Donald agreed, "that's why farmers in Afghanistan raised opioids because of drought. They were easier to grow and sell to the rest of the world. They had a much higher selling price, especially with regard to heroine addiction. Russia invaded, but we helped defend Afghanistan. We with Europe persuaded the Taliban to grow less opioid, but after al-Qaeda attacked us and we counterattacked, a new corrupt government emerged. Afghanistan became the world leader of causing heroine addiction. Millions of lives have continually been lost."

"I'd rather grow tomatoes," Peter replied.

"You can bring the cost down with the use of solar energy," Donald added. "You're close to a lake. There are fishing streams nearby. Down in the soil of those mountains are natural aqueducts. You can have all the water needed. Just use it in a useful way, and you'll have solar energy to help make it happen."

"Are you sure about that?" Peter asked with a crinkled nose.

"If you drive an electric car," Donald replied, "it can be charged by solar panels and wind turbines on a rooftop. I have all I need to power my house, and I sell some of it to the city to cover my water cost."

Peter stood shaking his head in doubt.

"Well, I reckon I'm going to need to grow a lot with all those other landowners coming to be my competition."

"You'll have all the credit you need to grow what you need," Donald assured him. "You're just the start of a much bigger project. Solar powered trucks will bring you water and take what you grow back to the city for them to sell. If it's cheaper for people to eat more or to save for other stuff, it'll enrich the economy."

"What more do I need to get a good start?"

"Lots of insects could help," Donald answered.

Peter gazed at Donald.

"They're a food source for countless people," Donald responded. "They have been for thousands of years. Billions of people outside the US still eat them."

"I don't know of anyone eating them."

"It's not as allowable here in the US, but it's common elsewhere. Per size, they have more protein than larger animals. They're a valuable source of that nitrogen. Even if you don't feed on them, they're a good compost source."

"Aren't they contagious?"

"Some of them can be. Some protect themselves with contaminants. Be aware if they're of a bight color, like red, orange or yellow. You might need to cook others to disinfect them if you get them in a contaminated environment.

"What are good ones to have?"

"Worms are good. Even though honey bees can be eaten, they're better off as pollinators. Crickets consume seven times less than cattle, as per weight, and caterpillars are a real good source of protein. Grasshoppers and ants can be plentiful."

"You sure would need to eat a lot of them," Peter replied shaking his head.

"That's their downside. They're more needed here as fertilizer."

"Where and how am I going to get them?"

"They'll need to be fed and kept in a place where they can stay and multiply."

"I need to be in a place where I'll be able to stay and have all I need," Peter replied showing his hands up to his shoulders.

"You're going to have plenty of company to work with," Donald reminded him.

"They're my competitors."

"You'll need to cooperate in ways to succeed."

"How's that possible?" Peter bellowed.

"There're plenty of ways," Jack assured him.

"What are they?" Peter was quick to ask.

"Do you know what you can use to get more carbon?" Jack asked.

"No, I don't," Peter answered.

"It's carbon," Jack informed. "Carbon bonds with carbon in multiple forms depending on their energy levels. The carbon in plants attracts the atmospheric carbon by means of photosynthesis. With air purifiers you can get carbon and water out of the atmosphere to help lower the temperature and stop climate change."

"Isn't there little water in the atmosphere over here?"

"Yeah, but you shouldn't be adding to it."

"Why's that?"

"Like what I had just demonstrated, water absorbs lots of heat. More of it in the atmosphere isn't good."

"What can I do?"

"Don't let it evaporate. Like in those compost bins, if they are also inside a container receiving light similar to sunshine, it'll be saved. More water can similarly be kept in containers and be purified with the use of solar energy.

12
THREAT ARRIVES

With Donald helping out in Summer Lake, and with Darcy in the hospital, Kayla had the house to herself.

It was an adventurous plan of James purchasing lots at Summer Lake to donate to qualified homeless campers, conditional to them not being addictive to drugs, and for them to be willing to combat climate change. He even purchased electric vehicles to transport essential items for greenhouse development. Self enforcement of such a condition was the need of those items for greenhouse development. However, the donations were not without risk. An expense from James' bank account was likely noticeable by account owners it had been stolen from.

A car parked in front of an RV on the side of an otherwise empty street. A shorter fellow got out on the passenger side while a taller fellow got out on the driver side. They went up to the side door of the RV.

"Greg," the tall guy hollered while pounding loudly on the door.

"Hi Paul," Greg said after he opened the door. "What's up?"

"This guy with me came here to find James Baker. Do you know where he is?"

"What's he done?"

"Do you really want to know?" the short guy asked with an angry stare.

"It must be serious," Greg gestured shaking his hand that faced them, "whoever you are."

"Just call me Rob."

"Okay Rob, I'm either in or out."

"He hacked into and stole from an account," the so-called Rob replied. "If you know what he might be up to, you need to tell us?"

"It's been awhile. He seems to have some guy helping him, and I believe he's peddling jewelry for the guy in turn. He's no longer buying drugs as far as I know."

"Where is he?" Rob loudly asked. "We need to find him or we're all going down."

"Is it that bad?"

"It's worse."

"I don't know for sure, but I believe the guy who's helping him got thrown into the river by a football player who was arrested but released with no charge for being an All-American."

"Was the player doing drugs?"

"He probably was. I heard there's an anonymous donor promoting some kind of charity project at Tommy's Inn. It could be James, and the football player is probably part of it."

"Thanks. We'll check it out," Rob replied as he turned to walk away.

"There's more you should know," Greg said.

Rob turned and stood in wait.

"I heard James was involved with someone else that went off a bridge into the river. They found a girl, not a guy. She somehow survived, and I believe she's helping James purchase all that stuff, and all of them are being controlled by the guy supposedly helping James. You can find James after finding her, but you still need to find whoever's controlling all of them."

"Is she a computer nerd?" Rob asked.

"Maybe, I don't know; why?"

"Because," Rob bellowed, "it's doubtful that James knows how to hack into bitcoin accounts that are privately owned and secretly used by such national leaders as even that one in Russia. Someone has found a way to do it. It must be a computer nerd. Bitcoin is being stolen and it's not known how it's being done. Where it's done is most likely here where strange things have been going on."

"The guy you're after must've had the other guy thrown in the river. It's likely the football player had been coerced to do it. The girl was probably covering for him, but I heard she got fired from working at Tommy's Inn for getting him into trouble. Most likely she was in need of help, and the guy you're after likely uses both her and James. Find her and you'll find James and then that guy."

"Thanks. We'll check it out."

The two fellows walked back to the car. The so-called Rob seated himself on the passenger side and Paul seated himself behind the wheel.

"We now have a lead," Rob said while holding his cell phone up in front of his mouth. "We're on our way to check it out."

Paul pushed buttons on his cell phone.

"It's on Franklin Boulevard near the university," he said. "It must be a new place."

He drove to and parked at the inn. They got out of the car and entered the dining room of the inn where Wanda Sue was serving only one customer.

She walked up to greet them.

"Hello. Where would you like to sit?"

"We're looking for a James Baker," Rob said. "He inherited a fortune, and there's a ten grand reward for whoever helps us find him."

"Wow," Wanda Sue blurted. "I've heard that name. I believe he was doing drugs, and I suspect he might be a generous donor financing a social group taking on climate change. I don't know why, but he's keeping his name secret for some reason."

"Do you know a Kayla?" Paul asked. "We've heard she worked here, was laid off and is now helping the donor."

"Yeah, she was just laid off for getting involved with something that would tarnish the reputation of this place, but it was just an accident and not her fault."

"Where can we find her?" Rob asked.

"There's a reporter over there," Wanda Sue said pointing at George, "who has reported on her dating a football player. He'd be interested in the reward thing, I'm sure."

"What's the player's name?" Paul asked.

"Bard Sucrets," Wanda Sue answered. "He's an All-American."

"Thanks," Rob said as he followed Paul over to the table George was sitting at.

"I heard you're interested in Bard Sucrets," Rob said as he stood beside and faced George. "Do you know where we could find him?"

"He should be at Autzen stadium practicing with the team."

"Where's it at?" Paul asked.

"Just go west on Franklin Boulevard all the way to the bridge on the right where it emerges with Coburg road. Take the first right after crossing the bridge. Take the first right after that, and the first left after that. You'll come to it on this side where you can park at the rear of the stadium."

"Do you have a photo of him?" Paul asked.

"What's this about?" George asked.

"I'm looking for a story as well," Rob again lied. "The New York Times is interested in this one of yours. You'll get credit and recognition."

George picked up his cell phone and pushed its buttons. He showed Rob its screen. Bard's photo appeared on it.

"I heard he's dating a girl of the name Kayla," Paul said.

"She lives close to Autzen Stadium," George revealed.

"We thank you very much," Rob said. "We'll let you know what we come up with."

"That'd be nice," George replied.

The two fellows walked back out to their car and drove it to Autzen Stadium, parked across the street from it and sat waiting. A girl riding a bicycle approached from the other direction. She turned left onto the bike path."

"That's most likely Kayla," Rob said.

Guys started coming out of Autzen Stadium. The likely players were getting on electric bicycles and crossing the street to the bike path.

"There's Bard," Rob said pointing at him.

Paul stared at the rearview mirror.

"It looks like we're going to have to get rid of a reporter," he said still staring at the rearview mirror.

George was sitting behind the wheel of his car that had parked behind them.

"Let's see," Rob replied. "We came west to turn north and then east. That bike path goes south. Kayla and Bard must be meeting at the inn. We need to stay out of the limelight. We'll just investigate behind the scenes while someone else rents a room at the inn. This'll be over in no time."

"Do we have more help?" Paul asked.

"We're to wait and find out all we can. This is too important to foul up, and they're sending us lots of backup along with a needed plan. For now, let's go back to that RV and have him find us a good place to hide."

13
REHIRED

Kayla hadn't gone to the inn. She had continued along a pathway straight to Franklin Boulevard after crossing the bridge. She then crossed Franklin Boulevard to where Oregon University was on the other side. The hospital was only a few blocks west of it. She continued on to visit her mother.

"Hello," Darcy said when Kayla walked into the room. "Is Donald still at Summer Lake?"

"Yes," Kayla replied, "he'll be there a couple more weeks."

"You must have the house all to yourself. Is your boyfriend seeing you there?"

"No."

"Did you two break up?"

"No. We just have other things to do."

"I don't think it's a good idea of you being all alone in the house. Why don't you want to see Bard anymore?"

"I'm just over my head and don't want to get him into anymore trouble."

"I'm sure he's capable of handling it."

"I'm sorry. I don't like telling you this. I'm involved in something that could be dangerous for him as well as me. I don't want to be doing it, but the circumstances were too overbearing at the time, and I have someone else helping me out that I can't let down."

"Exactly what are you involved in?"

"I'm an undercover spy for the FBI. I don't want to put Donald or you in danger. The owner of the inn wants me to return tomorrow to be in charge of rooms expected to fill up at the start of football season. He apologized for laying me off when I was there having dinner with Bard. I told him I understood why he did it, but I didn't tell him or Bard that I don't want to see Bard anymore."

"Are you spying on the guy claiming to have the hummingbird drones, or is it the guy that tried to rape you?"

"It's both of them, but we now trust each other."

"Oh, dear, you are in big trouble."

"Technically I am, but they're not the threat. The real threat is yet to come. It's why I don't want to see Bard anymore. It's putting his life in too much danger. The guy I'm supposedly spying on seems more worried of late."

"You need to get more help."

"Sorry, I'm in over my head."

Darcy squeezed her eyes tight as she laid flat on her back.

"Hey," Kayla said, "I'm confident the alien is able to protect me with his advanced technology."

"Who is he? Where did he come from? Is he from outer space?"

"I don't know for sure. He might actually be from inner space. Bard's friend Jack is majoring in physics and biochemistry. He explained to us how there can be worlds within worlds."

"I don't know what to believe anymore. You did get my hospital bill paid. I just now need to get my mind in order, and this isn't helping."

"Well, I'll let you have some time to do it. I'm going to the inn to have a late lunch with Bard. It's going to be tough telling him it's over, but it needs to be done."

"Does he know about your involvement?"

"He knows some of it. I should tell him everything. They might want to use him to get at me. He should have company everywhere he goes, and I should make sure he has earrings and a necklace with him."

"Take care; I hope it all gets sorted out in a way you and Bard get back together."

"I do as well," Kayla replied while turning to leave, "see you later."

When she arrived at the inn, she took notice of a couple of guys sitting in the front seat of a car. She put her bicycle in the bike rack and locked it, and then continued on into the diner.

She was approached by Mr. Olsen.

"Where's Wanda Sue?" Kayla asked.

"She passed out and is recovering in one of the rooms. Bard also passed out. He was here having dinner, and he was taken to the hospital."

"What?" Kayla asked with a fixed gaze.

"We had a bunch of new tenants," Mr. Olsen explained. "There were a lot of them to feed. I believe something got into the food Wanda Sue and Bard were testing for them."

"Did anyone else pass out?"

"No. One of them claimed to be a medic. He said Bard ate too much of it and needed to be rushed to the hospital.

He and his buddies carried him out. Wanda Sue seems to be recovering, but she should have the night off. Do you mind covering for her?"

"I don't have anything else to do, and I need to know what's going on."

She didn't believe they took Bard to the hospital, and she feared they would only come back to get her, but that she would have a better chance at the inn rather than being home alone.

Mr. Olsen went back to his office. She went to sit behind the counter. She was wearing both her earring and necklace when a man entered the main door of the inn.

"I'd like to rent a room for the night," he said.

"It's a hundred dollars," she replied while pointing at a note pad for him to register.

He filled it out and then handed her a hundred dollar bill.

"Do you mind showing it to me?" he asked.

"It's right down the hall on the right," she replied.

"I need some information. I'm sure you know where everything is around here."

She shrugged and led him down to the room instead of handing him the key. She unlocked the door for him.

"Please go on in," he said. "I need a little time to discuss what I'm looking for."

She was hesitant but led the way into the room. She crossed her arms and stared at him with her mouth open after he closed the door.

"I'm just a messenger," he said facing her. "I mean you no harm, but you're somehow involved in a scheme that's illegal. I'm sure we can work something out."

"I'm being used," she replied staring at him. "I have no control over it."

"Let me know who is controlling you and it'll be taken care of."

"He claims to be an alien stranger belonging to a secret society. That's all I know. He keeps most everything secret."

"How's he controlling you?"

"He hacked into my bank account, and he's using it against me. I went to the police, but they weren't able to do anything about it."

"How's he doing it?"

"I don't know," she blurted.

She suddenly had an idea.

"He could be hacking into your account. You should check it out."

He shrugged smirking. She nodded yes. He reached into his pocket for his cell phone, and he pushed its buttons.

In squeezing his eyes tight, he appeared not to believe what he just heard.

"Ten trillion dollars," he blurted. "It's from the Federal Treasury."

"You must be the richest guy on Earth," she replied, also being surprised by what she heard, "and you must have lots of clout with the government."

She did not have full control of the situation, but it was a moment when she appreciated the help.

"How are you doing this?" he asked leaning forward and staring at her.

"I'm not doing anything," she replied with a shrug. "It must be the secret society. I guess you're now a member as

I am. Maybe they're done with me. That'll sure be nice; nice for me anyway."

"What can I do about it?" he asked staring at her.

"I went to the police and told them everything I could. It seemed to help. At least it got me off the hook. They gave me immunity."

He rested his elbow on the table and placed his forehead in the palm of one hand, and then pointed his other hand at his chest and then at his ear, and finally at Kayla's chest.

Kayla nodded pointing at her chest, realizing he was wired and likely being controlled by someone as well as she was.

"They have Bard Sucrets," he warned. "He'll be crippled for life if you don't fully cooperate. They want to know where to find James Baker and the hacker of their treasury."

"Who are they?" she asked with a sneer.

"They are hired investigators just like I am. I was hired by them not realizing what I was getting involved with. They'll do what it takes to get what they want. They'll even cripple the star football player, and it'll only be a first step in gaining advantage, as they believe your caring for him is the weakness they'll need to use against you. They don't have such a weakness. They care not whether he lives or dies, or even what happens to me."

Staring angrily at him she put her fists on her chest and jerked them apart. He responded by putting his fists on his chest before shaking his head no.

"It's pointless," he assured her.

She felt helpless in fearing for Bard's safety. Her noble caring was a weakness she could not change for the better, and she felt guilty for it being her fault that Bard's career and life were now at stake.

"You know you can be arrested and charged for hacking into and stealing from the treasury, don't you?" she asked.

"I'm already as good as dead just because I know too much. I'm just a middle man hired to deliver the message. I'm now a witness. If I go to the law, my family will be killed."

"I'm the same, but I also care about what'll happen. Please don't let them hurt Bard. I'll do whatever they want if they first let him go."

He shook his head no.

"You need to convince them that you really can and will help. If you don't, they won't have anymore use for him. They'll waist him just for using him as an example. Anymore friends and family will next be in line, as mine are now."

"What do they want me to do?"

"They'll find you tomorrow," he replied after appearing to listen to someone else. "You need to ride your bike as far as you can east of the bike trail on the other side of the river. Without notifying the police or anyone else, don't resist. They'll take you to where they're keeping Bard. That'll be between you and them. As for me, I now need your cooperation. I know too much. Although the police could protect me, they can't protect my family, and they'll pay the price for your non cooperation."

"I reckon you're not calling the police," Kayla said with her frowning face facing the floor. "I'm not calling them either, but you're now my enemy. I reckon the only way of saving your family is if you die instead. Just thank me for having given you the medicine you needed to save your family."

He gazed with a crinkled nose at her.

She crossed her lips with her finger, picked up her cell phone and pushed 911 buttons. He tried to take it away from her. She jerked it back quick enough and spun around ducking under his arms. She backed up and sprayed him with something in the pen-like device she had in her hand.

He covered his eyes with his hands and staggered about.

"What did you spray me with," he yelled out and then stared wide eyed at her.

"Oh," she calmly replied, "just something for you to pass away with no pain. I didn't want to hurt you. I'm going to be on my bike heading east tomorrow morning, but I'm not helpless. They can have me for Bard. They'll have to let him go."

He was on his knees nearly passed out as she pushed 911 buttons.

"This is an emergency number," Kayla heard, "What and where is the problem?"

"A tenant here at Tommy's Inn just had a heart attack," she said with the phone in front of her. "I think he's dead. He passed out on the floor and is barely breathing."

After hearing that an ambulance would soon be on its way, she hung up.

"Did you block the signal?" she thought to ask.

"It is now blocked," she then thought.

She crossed her lips with her finger, but she then flipped her hand away from her mouth.

"Don't worry," she said to the guy facing her. "The signal is blocked. They're not hearing us."

He fell all the way to the floor with his eyes still open.

"They now have two of us to contend with," she continued informing him. "They need your cooperation as well as mine, but you need to cooperate with the police."

"No," he replied along with a sigh of relief. "You might have lied."

"Even if I did, you have little choice. I didn't lie, and your best option to save your family and yourself is to cooperate with the police. Lie down and pretend. It's yours and your families only hope."

He seemed to have passed out.

"Did he get my message?" she thoughtfully asked. "He got your message," she was thoughtfully assured.

Kayla walked out of the room to meet with medics that were soon to arrive. Thomas Olsen came out of his office when he heard the siren.

"Did something happen?" he asked.

"A new attendant is having a heart attack," she replied while opening the front door.

She led the medics to the room where the guy was lying on the floor with his eyes closed. Although the medics examined him and found no irregular body signs, they lifted him onto a stretcher and carried him out to the ambulance.

"What's going on?" Mr. Olsen asked.

"That was the new attendant having a heart attack. That's all I know."

"Boy, things sure happen with you around," he said while turning around to walk back to his office.

"He must've eaten some of that testable food," she reminded him.

He shook his head walking away.

Kayla noticed George approaching her. She crossed her lips with a finger. He nodded.

"You need to tell your detective friend right away that that guy claims he's being used, and he needs to be reported as dead. They have Bard. If they find out the police have been notified, they'll cripple him for life or just kill him. Please tell Detective Bentley right now. I'm sure she'll comply."

He nodded yes and walked away pushing buttons on his cell phone.

14
A PLACE TO HIDE

Kayla's dayshift at Tommy's Inn had ended. While riding her bicycle home and approaching the bike bridge, she saw the hummingbird and continued on across the bridge.

She saw James on the bike path holding a pistol. She stopped with one foot on the ground while he walked up close to her and offered to hand it over.

She shook her head no and flipped her hand forward. He pointed the pistol at himself while holding it by its barrel.

"Sorry," she apologized, "I don't want it. My dad was killed by one when I was fourteen. He was in bed with another guy's wife. They both had guns. My dad lost. He was trespassing for it to be no more than self defense."

James waved his hand forward for her to follow him. She walked behind him with her bicycle by her side. He led her to a bushy area where he then reached inside his pocket for a small tablet device. When he pushed its button, an area of the ground rose up. An elevator appeared.

She hid her bicycle within bushes and followed Bard on into the elevator. It lighted up after it lowered below ground level. It continued to lower to finally stop in front of a passage way into a room.

There were floor like beds and other essentials for cooking and storing food, and she noticed a large battery partway inside a wall.

"It's a diamond battery," James said facing it. "It can last more than five hundred years."

"It would be needed for space travel," Kayla replied. "Being able to turn yourself off for hibernation could also be an asset."

"That makes sense," James replied.

"Why did you bring me here? Are we leaving Earth?"

"I was informed of your calling for an ambulance. It was risky. They're waiting for you at Autzen Stadium, and they probably know where you live."

"I figured as much and was expecting help. They want me to lead them to you so you can lead them to the alien stranger. We'd then all be killed. I just considered the alien stranger was the better option with his advanced technology."

"He seems to be going along with what you're up to."

"Is he close by?"

"I have no idea. He probably has ways to all kinds of places."

"Do you know if he knows where they took Bard?"

James shrugged.

"My clothes must be hybrid pajamas as well as street clothes," she said shaking her head with a crinkled nose.

"It should only be for the night. One way or another it'll be over tomorrow after you go do what they asked of you, and you'll have to lead them here. I'm agreeing to it. Hopefully the alien is willing to somehow save us, but I don't know what I can tell them."

"We need to come up with something."

"I'll help in anyway I can."

"I appreciate it, and I respect you for risking your life in helping me save Bard."

"Yes, I'm willing to help, and I'm still willing to give you my gun if you change your mind."

"I trust you now. You've changed a lot."

"Nutrition has helped a lot, especially Korean ginseng. It renormalizes the immune system. A Korean gave me a root he cured with alcohol. I ate it and drank the alcohol. I didn't get high. I was alert and more responsive than I've been in a long-long time. I use ginseng tea bags. It collects in my body for a much longer time of effect."

"Well, Donald would sure like to know about that. What can we do down here besides sleep for the night."

"I have ways to disguise myself. You can do it too. We could go somewhere on foot."

Kayla reached for her phone and found it to have no dial tone.

"I'd like to talk to Detective Bentley about a good strategy. We could need her help and it'll be good to keep her informed. Can you call out from down here?"

"I never have. There's a particular signal that the drones can detect. My device sends it. They'll send back an image on its screen. That way I know whoever's in the area for me to go back up without being noticed."

"I suppose other signals are blocked in order for them not to be detected."

James nodded and walked over to where he put on a wig along with fake eyeglasses and a fake beard. He also happened to have a wig for Kayla and other fake eyeglasses.

All his clothes were too large for Kayla to wear, but she managed to come up with a blouse and skirt out of some leftover fabric.

James handed her an electronic tablet.

"Use this for your way in and out. You only have to push an area on the screen for you to see where you want to go. It'll indicate whether or not the path is clear."

"I just want to go somewhere I'll be able to talk to Detective Bentley. My phone could likely be bugged. Do you have one I can use?"

"I do, and it's not in my name."

He walked over to a bedded area and came back with a phone.

The screen indicated there was nobody outside anywhere near. They went back up in the elevator and then walked further away from the bike path.

She was still wearing both her earrings and necklace.

"Can you connect me with Detective Bentley," she thought.

"Police station," she heard someone answer the phone after about a minute.

"I'm lost and someone is stalking me. I was warned by Detective Bentley about him. Is she available?"

"She's off duty. I'll call and ask."

Kayla waited.

"Hello," she finally heard Detective Bentley's voice. "I'm Detective Bentley. Are you Kayla?"

"This is Kayla. Did you get the message?"

"I did. What do you want me to do?"

"I'm being taken captive by them tomorrow to where they're probably keeping Bard. I was informed they're near my home where they've been waiting for me to be back at home from work. They want me to help them find James and the guy that's been helping him. I'll try to lead them to the bike path that's just south of Autzen Stadium. I believe it's our best chance of saving Bard and everyone else."

"You could be killed. Are you willing to risk it?"

"I am."

"Is there a particular time?"

"It'll be sometime tomorrow morning. If you interfere, they'll do something to Bard."

"How can I help?"

"I'm sure we'll have help from someone else I know. He has hummingbird drones that'll call and let you know where we're going, and they might even help by sedating the enemy."

"Thanks for informing me, and I'll pass it on to the FBI agent. I'm sure he can get us all the help we'll need. After all, Bard's stature makes it a top priority."

"Thanks!"

"I'm sure we'll have even more help," Kayla thought after hanging up.

15
TO THE RESCUE

The next morning Kayla was on her bicycle peddling in the direction she had been instructed to go. She was on the west side of the river heading east to meet up with Bard's captives.

She shivered when she saw a guy on a bicycle coming from the opposite direction, but it was a false alarm. He continued past her.

Continuing east she was suddenly confronted by a large goose coming out of a bushy area closer to the fiver. It walked across the bike path right in front of her. She slowed to allow it to cross with no altercation.

"Watch where you're going," she shouted.

She continued on through the wooded area until she came to an open field where the bike path merged with a street. It was a back road with little use. A car passed by her and suddenly came to a stretching halt right in front of her.

She squeezed the break handles, but the bicycle slid to still hit the car and tumble to the ground. Feeling pain of her bruised shoulder, she managed to get up onto her feet and show her phone to two men that had gotten out of the back of the car and rushed approaching her.

One of them grabbed her phone away from her and reared back his arm to throw it.

"Wait," she shouted while reaching out to block the throw. "I need it to contact the guy you want to find."

"Why's that?" the guy with the phone in his hand asked with a mean stare.

"It's the only way I'll be able to contact him. He hides and doesn't let anyone know where he stays."

He grabbed her arm forcefully and pulled her to the back door of the car that had been left open. He shoved her onto the seat. She sat up only to become locked in between the two guys.

The guy with her phone handed it to a guy sitting in the front passenger seat who had a monitor.

"It's not wired," he said after he examined the monitor, "and it's turned off."

The guy who had handed him the phone flipped his hand forward. The car accelerated to a high speed.

"Let's not get pulled over," the passenger side guy warned.

Kayla slightly nodded with a little hope. She was not wired except for diamond earrings she had pinned within her hair out of sight, and for the necklace she hid behind her blouse.

She decided to pick their brains.

"I sure miss Bard. Is he still alive?"

They did not answer.

"He is still alive," she thought.

"Did you hurt him?" she asked.

They did not answer.

"He is not hurt," she thought.

"Where is he?" she asked.

"Shut up," the driver yelled.

She shrugged appearing sad.

"He is inside a motor home where they are taking you," she finally thought. "They intend to kill you and Bard after they succeed with the information they expect you will provide them with if it turns out to be true, and after I and James are captured and killed as well."

They entered the town of Springfield on the east side of Eugene wherefrom they turned right onto a street heading south to the main one-way street heading out of town east. When they passed a small town called Vida, they came to a camping area beside the McKenzie River. Two RVs and several campers filled the camping area with no other room for any other campers. They stopped the car in front of an RV.

The man sitting on the right side of her got out and led her to the door of that RV, and she noticed a hummingbird hovering nearby it. She had hope.

"Get in there," he loudly told her.

She opened the door and entered the RV to see Bard lying on the floor. His arms were tied behind his back, and with three men sitting in padded chairs in front of him. The one closest to him held a club waving it at Bard's knees. Bard shrugged and pointed a finger at his ear.

Kayla nodded. Bard nodded back.

One guy pointed at an empty chair. She sat down only to be approached by one of the men.

"Tell us what you know," the muscular man standing in front of her said. "Your boyfriend's life depends on it."

"I only know where there is a secret location of a Secret Society that's using me," Kayla said with eyes covered by a hand. "That's all I know."

"Where is it?"

"It's underground near a football stadium."

"How do we find it?"

"Its exact location is too difficult to describe. It's in a wooded area and covered by ground in order for it not to be found. Why I was trusted to know where it is I have no idea."

"Well, then, you'll have to show us the way. My two buddies here will escort you."

"I need my phone."

"Now, why would you need your phone?"

"The hideout is a meeting place. My phone is needed to call James Baker. He's a member of a secret society, and he can take you to its leader."

"It probably has a tracer," one of the sitting men warned. "Besides, she killed one of our guys. She's dangerous."

"It's a special phone that they'll only answer if they can hear it's my voice. One of the guys bringing me here checked it out. It has been turned off for not being traced. Besides, I'm aware of you knowing of its potential."

"Use this," he said with phone in hand.

"It won't work. Mine has this secret number that's set on redial. I don't know what it is."

"She could be telling the truth," one of the guys said. "They do have advanced capability. They somehow figured out how to hack into bitcoin accounts.

"Where's your phone?" the muscular man asked while staring down at her.

"The guy that checked it out in the car must have it," she replied.

"Go get her phone," the muscular man ordered.

One of the men stood up from his seat. He left the RV to soon return with her phone. He handed it to the muscular man.

"If it's being traced," the muscular guy said, "you're All-American is good as dead."

"I know that, but I need the phone in order to call James."

"What's his number?"

"I don't know. As I already said, I push redial to a secret number. I talk and hang up. If I get a ring back, I'll push the redial again. It tells him to meet me at the meeting place. If I receive another ring, then he'll be there."

"Do it," he ordered handing her the phone.

She pushed the redial.

"Hello," she said and hung up.

The phone began ringing. After it stopped, she again pushed the redial and hung up. It began ringing again.

"He'll be there only if I get there in time."

"Take her outside and show her a little persuasion," the muscular man said.

"He'll know something's going on if I don't get there within an hour," Kayla replied.

She and Bard faced each other with frowns.

"I love you," she sincerely said, "and I'm here to save you."

"I love you too," he sincerely replied, "and I believe you really want to. Risking your life for me isn't good, but you need to do exactly what they want."

"Do to me whatever you want," she replied facing the muscular fellow, "but if I'm not there within an hour, James will know something's going on. I don't want Bard to get hurt. One of your guys will need to notify you after we get there. I'll still need to know Bard's okay."

The muscular guy hesitated staring at her.

"Take her back out to the car and tell those guys to take her back. She has an hour to save her boyfriend. If James isn't there, she'll have to be wasted."

Bard squeezed his eyes shut.

Two guys stood up and escorted her to the car. Its driver got back in. She sat up front on the passenger side to direct him while the other three guys sat in the back.

She directed the driver to the football stadium.

"Park here," she said.

The driver parked the car.

"Follow me," she said while getting out of the car. "We need to go up the bike path."

"Take her," the driver said with phone in hand. "I'm staying here to make sure it's not a trap."

She and the three guys in the back seat got out of the car. She led the way along the bike path. A bicyclist came their way. They stood in his way.

"Can I get by," he asked after stopping, "or is something going on I need to know about?"

Kayla faced the guys and shrugged.

They stepped aside and let him continue on his way. They themselves then continued with Kayla guiding them a little farther on the path. Kayla pointed toward bushes.

"I have something to show you," she said in response to their frowning faces.

She led them to the elevator location.

"Why are we here?" one of the guys asked, as the others guys faced away with guns in their hands.

"You'll soon find out," she replied.

The elevator rose above ground.

"Take her down," one guy said. "I'm staying to make sure it's not a trap. If he's down there, one of you come up and tell me. I'll let the boss know."

She and two guys entered the elevator, and it lowered. They walked into the room with one of them holding Kayla's arm and pointing a gun at her head while the other guy pointed a gun at James who was wearing earrings.

"You need to tell us where to find your guy," the guy pointing the gun at James said. "Yours and hers lives depend on it."

"Don't tell them anything until I know Bard is okay," Kayla warned.

"You know I won't," James agreed. "I know you're willing to die for him, and I am too."

"Take her back up there, the guy with the gun said after pushing buttons to find no dial tone."

The guy close to her pointed at the elevator. They walked back into it. It rose. They walked out of it."

"He's down there," the guy with her said. "I think he'll cooperate."

The guy made the call.

"You have just another hour," he said after hanging up.

"What can I do?" she asked.

He faced the guy that came back up with her.

"You two need to go back down there and get him to come up here and talk."

He went back down and came back up with James and the other guy.

"Times running out," the guy with the phone said. "If you're no good to us, we'll just have to waste you. I'd finish you right here, but it'd be too easy on you."

She noticed a hummingbird hovering nearby.

"Follow me," James replied.

He led the way. They walked towards the car, but the driver was missing when they arrived. The guy pointed his gun at Kayla.

"Get in. I'll drive."

A hummingbird suddenly hovered between them and sped away. He turned his head to see it and soon passed out on the ground.

Police cars suddenly surrounded them.

"I know where they're keeping Bard," Kayla said facing a policeman.

"He's been rescued," Detective Bentley said while standing between a guy in handcuffs and the FBI agent she had earlier consulted with.

The guy in handcuffs was the so-called Rob. She walked up to him.

"Where are you from?" Kayla asked.

"None of your damn business," he replied.

"Who hired you?" she asked."

"None of your damn business," he replied.

"Where is he?"

"How do you know it's a he?" he asked with a smirk.

"Dwight Stevens hired him," Kayla replied. "He lives in Chicago."

"What the hell's going on?" he asked shaking his head. "You must know more than you let on."

"I'm psychic, and you're in big trouble after I inform Dwight you told us what he's up to."

"What do you want from me?"

"Not much: just to inform the law of everything you know what Dwight is up to."

"We think you for finding the guy," the FBI agent said. "Our nation is now a lot safer."

"You're welcome," she replied.

She noticed Bard getting out of a police car. He walked up to her.

"I love you," he said, "and I want to spend the rest of my life with you."

"What about your football?"

"We start the season with the number one team in the nation."

"If you win, I'll accept," she kidded, postponing the crowd celebration.

"I think she feels you need to concentrate more on the game," George suggested. "She's just given you a little more motivation."

Bard nodded with a wink.

16
THE GAME BEGINS

Kayla woke, dressed and went to approach Donald and Darcy sitting in the living room.

"Are we safe?" Darcy asked. "I see you wearing your earrings and necklace."

"We should be," Kayla replied. "James is now trusted by the alien stranger. No more being in charge of the charity donation I'm free to do whatever I want."

"What about the project at Summer Lake?" Donald asked. "Who's in charge of it?"

"James is, and there's no longer any need to steal to finance it."

"How'd they fix that?"

"It was mostly Wanda Sue's doing. She was able to set up a bond system. Those who want to seriously take on global warming are willing to invest. Bard's credit status helped get it going. Those bonds are selling. Hopefully it'll convince government it could do likewise. It needs to buy out those fossil fuel producers for them to have useable credit in solar energy."

"It could be a social security option for our retirement income," Donald noted, "to allow all investors the choice of allowing government to use insurance payments for purchasing a bond for the finance of solar energy."

"What are you up to today?" Darcy asked.

"Coach Molten gave me a free ticket to the game today. He's letting me and Wanda Sue watch the game in the booth."

"It's a tough opening game," Donald noted. "It's a big ten team favored to win it all. Hopefully it'll be an upset."

"I won't be upset," Kayla kidded as she waved goodbye and walked to the stadium. She noticed the hummingbird hovering nearby. She even noticed it when she entered the stadium and made her way to the booth.

"Do you see that hummingbird?" a fan asked pointing at it. "What's it doing inside the stadium?"

"I think it wants the ducks to win," Kayla kidded. "It prefers ducks over wolverines."

They both smiled. She then walked up to the booth.

"Coach Molten said I'm permitted to sit inside," she told the attendant. "I'm Kayla Chalet."

"She is," George told the radio announcer.

She seated herself beside George. He faced her.

"How are you and Bard doing?" he asked.

"I told him I'd only marry him if they win," Kayla answered.

Wanda Sue had just entered the both.

"I told Jack I'd marry him if he'd let me win at pool," she kidded.

"We're now working for the social club," Kayla said facing George. "It should be safe."

"It's not only safe," Wanda Sue replied, "it's going to be more profitable."

"I'd like to hear the details," George said.

"All I can say is that it's a legal setup," Kayla replied. "I'm sure Wanda Sue would like to fill you in."

He faced Wanda Sue. She nodded.

The radio announcer was on the air praising Bard for his ability to block, catch the football and to run past defensive players. The stadium had filled up with fans. Both teams were on the field. The game was soon to begin.

The ducks won the toss and elected to start on defense. The Wolverines decided to start on the twenty five yard line after the kickoff instead of running with the ball in an attempt for more yards. They then ran and passed their way to the goal line in six plays, and kicked and made the extra point.

After the kickoff, the Ducks started on their twenty-five. It was fourth and seven on the thirty yard line. They opted to kick a field goal that succeeded through the uprights.

It was a battle from there on. Bard ran for more than a hundred yards and a touchdown, and had caught two touchdown passes, but the Ducks were still behind by four points with less than three minutes left in the game. It was win-or-lose with no chance of an overtime period.

The Wolverines were on offense, being third down with eight yards to go on their own forty yard line. They elected to pass for first down. The quarter-back threw to an open receiver at the five yard line. The game would surely have been over if the ball had been caught, but Jack managed to intercept the pass and run back to their own forty yard line. They had sixty yard to score a touchdown and win the game.

The Ducks managed to drive the ball down to the Wolverines forty-five, but there was only five seconds left.

The quarter back was being rushed. He managed to through a screen pass to Bard, who managed to slip by a couple nearby tacklers and outrun all others into the end-zone for the win.

She had been able to hear a radio announcer praise Bard because of his abilities to block, run and catch the football. She had seen him outrun defensive players for the winning touchdown. She was now obligated to accept his proposal for marriage.

www.ingramcontent.com/pod-product-compliance
Lightning Source LLC
LaVergne TN
LVHW011949070526
838202LV00054B/4863